COFFEE & CORPSES

CONNIE CAFE MYSTERIES
BOOK 1

MAISY MARPLE

A
Connie Cafe
MYSTERY

ALSO BY MAISY MARPLE

Visit Maisy Marple's Author Page on Amazon to read any of the titles below!

Connie Cafe Series

Coffee & Corpses

Ligature & Latte

Autumn & Autopsies

Pumpkins & Poison

Death & Decaf

Turkey & Treachery

Mistletoe & Memories

Snow & Sneakery

Repairs & Renovations

Bagels & Bible Study

S'more Jesus

Proverbs & Preparations

Sharpe & Steele Series

Beachside Murder

Sand Dune Slaying

Boardwalk Body Parts

RV Resort Mystery Series

Campground Catastrophe

Bad News Barbecues

Sunsets and Bad Bets

Short Stories

Forty Years Together

Long Story Short

The Best Gift of All

Miracle at the Mall

The Ornament

The Christmas Cabin

Cold Milk at Midnight

Short Story Collections

Hot Cocoa Christmas

Unapologetically Christian Essays

Reason for the Season

God is Not Santa Claus

Free Will is Messy

Fear Not

Not About this World

We Are All Broken

Veritas

God Ain't Your Butler

An Argument for Hate

Agape Love (With Pastor Michael Golden)

<u>Addiction Help</u>

Hard Truths: Overcoming Alcoholism One Second At A Time

CONTENTS

1

A sliver of sunlight shot through the gap between my lavender blackout curtains and hit me square in the eyelids, forcing me to roll over and contemplate waking from my far too-short slumber.

I knew I had a busy day coming up, and it would only be to my benefit to get up early and start my day off with a warm shower, leisurely scripture reading and prayer time, and, of course, a steaming hot cup of bold black coffee, French roast, thank you very much.

I also knew that I had been up until two in the morning, daydreaming and writing down plans for my yet-to-exist business on scraps of yellow legal pad.

My name's Connie Cafe. Yes, that's my real last name. And don't think it hasn't messed with me.

For the longest time, as long as I can remember, in

fact, I've wanted to open up a coffee shop where people from miles around could come and sit down with a friend or loved one and enjoy a really great cup of coffee while they caught up on the latest happenings in their all too busy lives. It would be a place where people could go to slow down for an hour or two, a place where they could sit down and catch their breath and enjoy the scenery and the company of people they love.

That was my dream.

Unfortunately, it's still my dream. My life hasn't exactly gone according to plan. I'm thirty-five, single, but still searching for Mr. Right, and living with my mother. My father passed away when I was in college, which was a major factor in me not graduating. I dropped everything to come home and help my mother get through it all, and, well, I just never left.

I work as a freelance journalist for *The Coffee Creek Gazette*, the town's local paper - and I use the term 'journalist' loosely. Basically, I get an email from the paper's editor, Sheila Robinson, whenever there's anything semi-newsworthy going on in the quaint little town of Coffee Creek. Then I grab my camera and my phone and head out to interview someone about something that will be bound to make the middle or back page of the paper. I once made the front page when I wrote a story about a new church opening in town! It was a particularly slow week that week, so my story was the lead. In the past ten years, I've written about four thousand stories for them, all between 250 and 500 words, and all about local small-town things such as church openings, bake sales, county fairs, and summer safety. Nothing to write home about, I'm afraid.

That's my main job.

I also write books and publish them on the internet. Things haven't exactly taken off yet, but I can usually muster a few hundred dollars a month in book sales. Plus, I keep trying. That's what you're supposed to do, right?

Oh yeah, I also work at one of the world's largest coffee chains - mornings and weekends. They call us baristas, but I would hardly classify what I do as worthy of such a name. I make the drinks as I've been trained to make them, as was mandated by corporate. Still, it's good practice for me, for the day when I will be able to open up my own little place in town. And I can guarantee that my little place will have creativity in droves, and the best darn tasting coffee ever, plus, ambiance that isn't as sterile as a hospital operating room. When you come to my cafe, you'll feel like you're at home - only the coffee will be way better!

I decided it was time to get up. That sun wasn't going to go away anytime soon, and my day wasn't going to get any less busy with me hanging around in bed, dreaming about my future endeavors. If I wanted that coffee shop, I was going to have to get up and work.

I sat up on the edge of the bed, my lavender comforter (yeah, I have a thing for lavender) draped across my lap as

I wiped the sleep from my eyes and had one of those yawning stretches that just seems to wake everything up all at once.

My bare feet touched down on the old wooden floors, which were unusually cold for this late May morning. My mother and I lived in an old farm house on the outskirts of town.

The story is, my father had fallen in love with it the first time he saw it. My mother was indifferent, and just really wanted a place they could call their own. Like most young couples, they were sick of renting and were ready to take the plunge into home ownership.

My father saw the potential in this little place and they put in an offer that was accepted immediately. When my mother tells me that they got the house and forty acres of land for less than thirty thousand dollars, I still find it hard to believe. But, "those were the times," she always reminds me, "and this place was a fixer upper," she adds for good measure.

The remaining twenty years of my father's life was spent working on the house, tinkering and getting as many parts of it to his specifications as he could. He realized quickly that he didn't need forty acres of land because he wasn't a farmer. He just liked the house. The three acres that surrounded the house was kept by my parents, and they sold the remaining thirty seven acres off in smaller parcels. The money they made from the land went to paying off the house and renovations that my parents had deemed necessary.

I can't complain, it's a great house. But these cold wooden floors and even colder farmhouse windows were part of the original home that I continually wish my parents would have upgraded.

But they're, "too full of charm." That's my mother's opinion on the matter. And growing up with my father, I know that was his opinion, too.

As I shuffled my feet across the floor and grabbed my bathrobe, I was thankful that the bathrooms in the house had been upgraded, and that the shower was straight up luxury compared to the windows and the floors.

My two O'clock morning was hanging with me. I had to go wash it off and grab a cup of coffee, or this might be a much longer day than the clock would suggest.

"WELL, GOOD MORNING," my mother greeted me as I entered the kitchen. She was standing in the corner, next to the coffee pot, mug in hand, feet crossed, arms crossed, bright yellow apron draped down in front of a deep plum colored shirt and lime green jeans. Her bright red hair made her almost too bright to look at this early in the day.

"Good morning," I replied, as I walked over to the cupboard and grabbed a mug for myself. I looked at the mug in my hand, and then shot my mother a glance before putting it back and grabbing a bigger mug that was stashed away toward the back of the cupboard. "I think it's going to be this kind of day," I proclaimed, holding the big mug up with two hands as if presenting it to my mother for final approval.

My mother nodded. "I know what you mean," she chuckled. "Sometimes I wake up and turn this coffee pot on and think to myself, there's not enough coffee in the world for today."

"I hear ya," I nodded.

"What's your day looking like?" She asked, her feet beginning to tap rhythmically on the floor of the kitchen.

"The usual." I set my big honking mug down on the counter and pulled my phone from my back pocket, and opened up the calendar. "I have a meeting with Sheila at nine, then work at the coffee shop at ten, then work on whatever story Sheila gives me until dinner. After dinner, if I have any energy left, I'll write another chapter of the book I'm working on."

She nodded, shifting her weight and turning to get the first cup of coffee for the day. After her cup was full, she extended the pot to me. I grabbed my mug off the coun- tertop and held it out for her to fill up.

I watched and salivated as the steam rolled off the black waterfall that was running into my cup.

"Thanks," I said, raising my mug in my mother's direction as a sort of toast.

"To a good day." She winked and raised her cup in response.

We both brought our noses down to the rim of our mugs and took a ceremonial sniff of the elixir of life, one of the best creations God bestowed upon humanity.

2

After twenty minutes of scripture reading, my mind was centered, and my coffee mug was empty. I rinsed it out and set it down in the kitchen sink before grabbing my keys and laptop bag and heading for the car.

Living outside of town has been a great thing for mom and me. We don't live that far away from civilization, but that ten-minute drive at the beginning and end of my day can be really helpful. Plus, I do so many interviews and write so many articles for the paper that it's nice to have a little distance between us and everyone else.

As was typical, I arrived at Sheila's office a few minutes early. And as was typical, Sheila Robinson, editor of *The Coffee Creek Gazette,* was rushing around the tiny office. If someone didn't know what year it was, they would say that it looked like a woman from the nineties who went back in time to an office from the sixties and was trying to get a newspaper to run stories in 2020 about people who lived their lives like they were in the seventies.

Sheila was in her fifties and just a few years from retirement. She had big blond hair (dyed, no doubt), full of cascading curls that draped down her face, accenting her heavily applied blush and thick lipstick. Today she was wearing a floral print dress with huge shoulder pads.

"Oh, hi, Connie," she tossed out as she walked from one desk to another, a stack of papers in her hands. She set those papers down on the second desk and went back over to her desk to grab more. "I'll be right with you. You're not in a hurry, are you?"

"No more than usual," I replied, taking a seat on one of the chairs that were just inside the front door. This was what Sheila would call the 'Waiting Room'. But anyone who was standing in the office would more than likely just refer to them as the chairs inside the front door.

Jeff Toobin, the other 'field reporter' for *The Coffee Creek Gazette*, was sitting at his desk, which was the third and final desk in the office. It was located behind Sheila's desk, which was the desk that Sheila was in the process of uncovering. He wrote for the *Gazette* full-time, which allowed him to complete his writing from inside the office.

This is going to sound bad, but I felt kind of sorry for the guy. Sure, my writing only got me a few hundred dollars a week, but if I had to write my articles in this place with its drab brown carpet, wood-paneled walls, and drop ceiling, I'd surely go crazy.

"What's going on, Connie?" He called, raising a small styrofoam cup, steam rolling out of the top of it. His sneaker-clad feet were perched across the corner of his desk. A long pair of brown pants and a white button-up shirt with brown pin-stripes completed the ensemble of my tall and slender writing colleague. His shaggy mop of hair and Tom Selleck mustache made him look like he was an actual living part of the office.

"Not much, Jeff," I called over the top of our frantic boss, who was now in a full frenzy, blowing puffs of air through her lips to get her long, flowing locks of hair out of her face. "How about you?"

"Oh, you know," he said, bringing the coffee to his lips and taking a dramatically loud sip, exhaling emphatically as he put the coffee cup down on the edge of his desk. "Just living the dream."

Sheila stopped what she was doing and stared at Jeff. "Now, you cut that out. You and I both know there are far worse places to work than *The Coffee Creek Gazette*. Plus, you get to see me every day. Honestly, I should start charging you for this level of entertainment."

We all shared a chuckle at this. That was one thing about Sheila - she always looked flustered, but she knew it, and she knew how to have fun with it.

She looked back down to her desk and then slapped her forehead with an open palm.

"I've been looking for that piece of paper all morning long, and the whole time it was taped to the side of my computer screen!" She laughed as she looked in my direction. "Admit it, that's why you love me!"

"Absolutely," I smiled.

Sheila ripped the taped sheet of paper from her computer monitor and held it out to me.

"This is your assignment. I'll admit, it's not the most exciting, but it will give you an opportunity to learn something new about the world of high-stakes golf in Coffee Creek."

She smiled a sly smile as I stood up and took the paper from her hand. *Great*, I thought to myself. I couldn't think of anything I'd rather cover less - except, perhaps, for the sights and sounds of garbage pickup as seen through the eyes of a sanitation worker. That story would give me less excitement, yet, somehow, I thought it had the potential to be far more interesting.

"Excuse me," I said, studying the information on the paper, "did you say *high stakes* and *golf* and *Coffee Creek* in the same sentence?"

"I did." She nodded and smiled. I could tell she was doing her best to stifle a laugh.

"This is a thing?" I held the paper up, and a look of surprise and mild disdain washed over my face.

"It sure is a thing, ma'am. And I've already called the Pro Shop. They'll be expecting you sometime this afternoon."

"I really wanted that story," Jeff piped up from his desk. "Do you know what she's got me doing?"

"Pipe down," Sheila scolded. "You're lucky to work here, Jeff…remember?"

"Well," he said, taking another sip of his coffee. He stood up and grabbed his light brown jacket off the back of his chair. He walked by me and said, "It looks like I'm off to go see what a day in the life of a sanitation worker in Coffee Creek is really like."

I waited for the door to the office to slam behind him before I let out a most satisfying laugh.

"Count your blessings, young lady," Sheila smiled. "You could be that guy."

By the time I arrived at the coffee shop, the morning rush had already come and gone. A fact that Reba, my best friend at the shop, reminded me of every day.

"Brutal!" She called out as I came around the counter and put on my green apron. "It's absolutely brutal in the mornings without you."

"Sorry," I shrugged. "I can help you with the cleanup."

As I looked around the counter, it was clear that the morning had, in fact, been brutal. It was also clear that for as long as Reba had been working at the shop and handling the morning rush, she had not learned how to make coffee and clean up after herself at the same time.

Empty coffee pots were scattered along the back wall, on the counter, and next to a small sink. Two dirty blenders were in the sink, filled to the brim with water. The floor was covered with paper cups and tops that hadn't stayed in Reba's hand long enough for her to write the customers' names on them, and two spent markers were lying next to the cash register awaiting a proper burial.

Reba's in her late twenties and lives with her boyfriend Dillon. He's a bit of a neat freak. At least, that's what Reba tells me. I've never met him. She says he does all the cleaning, or at least most of it, so she doesn't have to bother.

When she's at work, I'm the one who swoops in after the morning rush to get the back area neat and tidy again.

"If you wouldn't mind," Reba said, biting her bottom lip in a playful way while batting her long eyelashes at me. Her blue eyes were piercing this morning, with her dyed purple hair was tied back in a tight ponytail.

"I don't mind at all," I smiled and got to work sweeping up the cups and swiping the markers into the trash. After that, I cleaned out the blenders and the coffee pots and then refilled a few of them for the pre-lunch coffee rush. That one wasn't nearly as busy as the early morning rush, but it certainly presented its challenges.

"So, what kind of juicy gossip are you working on

today?" Reba asked as I took a few last wipes at the counter with the damp cloth in my hand.

I put my hand on my hip and dropped my shoulders, feigning offense. "Gossip? Is that what you think I peddle in?"

"Pretty much," she nodded, a smirk forming across her lips.

"Has anyone ever told you that you can be a real jerk sometimes?"

She brought her index finger up to her chin and stared at the ceiling. "Let me think." She tapped her finger a few times against the side of her mouth and then brought her eyes down and focused them on me. Her finger shot forward in my direction. "You!" She exclaimed, laughing.

"Well, it's absolutely one hundred percent true," I chuckled.

I walked past her and placed the damp rag over the goose-necked sink faucet where it hung lifelessly.

"I'm actually not very excited about today's assignment," I began. "But, it pays the bills, I suppose. I have to go the *Coffee Creek Golf Club* and interview some golfers about the upcoming tournament and blah, blah, blah."

"Wow," Reba nodded. "Less than a sentence in, and you're already using the 'blah, blah, blahs'."

"You bet I am." I puffed out my chest and put both hands on my hips, striking a Supergirl pose as if to say, 'what are you gonna do about it?' Then all at once, I pushed every ounce of air out of my body and shriveled like a deflated holiday yard decoration, my head curling toward the floor. I zombie-walked over to Reba and put my head at rest on her shoulder, heaving my shoulders up and down as I fake-cried. "Seriously, though. I'm really going to hate this one."

She patted my back and whispered, "I'm sorry."

3

It was just after one when I left the coffee shop and got into my car to drive over to the *Coffee Creek Golf Club*.

I looked up and took note that the sky was a perfect shade of blue with big puffy white clouds moving slowly across it.

They were the kinds of clouds that I remember being so much fun from my childhood. My father and I would sit on the front porch, or we'd set up folding chairs in the backyard and just stare at the clouds for what seemed like hours.

He would always have a tall mug of steaming hot coffee, black as black could be.

"What's that one look like to you?" He'd ask me.

"A dragon," I'd call out, pointing my finger up at the

sky. "Don't you see it, daddy? There's his nose, and his claws, and his big tail."

"I do," he'd say, each time so astonished with what I'd been able to imagine.

He'd take a sip of his coffee and sit back and say, "You know, Connie; there might come a time in your life when you're no longer able to see the dragons in the clouds, you know? I hope that day doesn't come for you. But if it does, just remember that your daddy loves you, and even if you can't see the dragons in your clouds anymore, I can."

I didn't understand what he meant at the time, but I've spent a lot of years thinking about those days since he passed away. Now, I realize that he was telling me to think big, to imagine my life as something bigger than what the world would put in front of me. Anything is possible through hard work and undying devotion to God.

Looking up at the clouds now, I saw one that looked like a dragon. I could almost feel my father wrapping his arms around me, reminding me to dream big.

The first item I was going to put on the menu of my someday cafe would be called 'Daddy's Cup' - a tall mug of dark black coffee, steaming and full of love.

I wiped the tears that had formed from my eyes, started my car, and prepared to drive over to the golf club. A day like today would no doubt bring the golfers out in droves. I'd have plenty of people to interview.

And even though it didn't seem like much of a story,

and certainly not one that I wanted to write, it was one more step in the direction of my dream.

Work hard enough, and someday, your imaginary dragons will become your reality.

JUST AS I SUSPECTED, the parking lot was full of cars and golf carts. Most of the golfers appeared to be putting their clubs back into their cars. There were pockets of men and women gathered in small groups of three or four, having conversations, enjoying a laugh about what had just transpired.

Coffee Creek, being a small town, had a small Golf Club.

I walked up the sidewalk to the Pro Shop/Bar. To my left, there were four or five guys warming up around the practice putting green, no doubt waiting for their round to begin.

I reached the front door of the yellow-sided building that looked more like someone's small house than a place of business.

Upon entering, there was a thin green carpet that was showing the effects of years of wear. I walked through a dimly lit hallway. There were doors on either side of the hallway with cute signs for the bathrooms. The men's room had a male golfer in mid-swing, and the women's room had a female golfer in mid-swing. There was a sign dangling from the drop ceiling that read:

Men to the Left

<——————

Because Women are
Always
Right!

I really got a kick out of this sign. It reminded me of an expression my parents used to say to each other whenever my mother would ask my father to do something he didn't want to do. They'd say it in unison: "Happy Wife, Happy Life!" And then they'd both laugh, and my father would get up from whatever he'd been doing and go do whatever task my mother had requested.

As I passed the bathrooms, the hallway opened up into a large bar area. The bar started on one side of the wall and wrapped around a corner at a ninety-degree angle, where it ended on the other wall. Opposite the bar, there were thirty feet of floor-to-ceiling windows that gave a picturesque view of the eighth hole and all of the duffers struggling to hit good shots on that hole.

My father used to golf here. He said that if you misplayed number eight, you might as well not even stop in for a post-round drink. "Best to head straight to your car and save yourself some dignity."

Because I hadn't ever been to the course, I didn't know

what he was talking about or what he meant. But now, staring out the windows at the struggling foursome, it finally clicked.

There was a small crowd of guys gathered in front of the window, seven of them altogether, each with a beer in hand, laughing mercilessly at one bad golf shot after another.

Five more guys were sitting at the bar, watching a tiny TV that was mounted on the corner of the wall. They all had beers and sandwiches in front of them and were watching a televised golf tournament.

As I approached the bar, a few of them stopped chewing their sandwiches and put down their drinks, and stared at me.

I suppose I must've looked pretty out of place. For one, I was a female under the age of fifty. Two, I had a camera around my neck. And three, I was wearing a salmon-colored linen blazer and matching pants with a form-fitting white camisole.

Not exactly golfing attire.

And, if I do say so myself, I was looking rather fetching.

"Bogey!" Called a portly, balding man at the bar as he turned toward the window. "It looks like someone needs your help."

A rail-thin man wearing long, faded green trousers and a green and white striped polo turned and started walking toward the bar. His skin was as tan as any I'd ever seen.

He had a gold bracelet that dangled loosely on his wrist and made a noise not unlike the jingling of loose change as he walked. He was balding but had a comb-over so long that it had to be tucked behind his left ear.

The man walked directly past me and opened up a flip-up door that doubled as the part of the bar where waitresses might pick up drink orders if this were an actual restaurant.

When he was firmly on the other side of the bar, he turned and stood in front of a cash register that was about eight feet away from where I was standing.

"May I help you?" He asked, staring at me but refusing to move. I walked over to the register and looked at him, noticing for the first time how sharp and menacing his pale blue eyes were.

"Yes, actually," I said. It took me a moment to find my bearings in this place. "I'm Connie Cafe with *The Coffee Creek Gazette*. My editor, Sheila Robinson, said she's made arrangements for me to come out and interview some golfers about the upcoming tournament this weekend."

"I don't know nothing about that," he said, his voice harsh and uninviting.

I said a small prayer in my head in hopes that the good Lord would allow me to keep my patience and breathe through this wholly challenging situation.

"Is there any chance that my boss, Sheila, may have spoken to anyone else this morning?" I asked, trying my best to smile sincerely.

"Nope," he quickly replied, holding out his arms wide and gazing from one side of the room to the other. "I'm the only one here who answers the phones."

I didn't want to, but I found myself actually believing him. Sheila certainly wasn't one of the most organized people in the world. That much was for sure. Plus, this wouldn't be the first time that she'd forgotten to call ahead to let someone know that I was coming for an interview.

Just last year, I had to head out to a house a few miles outside of town. I was interviewing Phyllis Kirch about her world-famous blueberry crumble. Truth be told, it wasn't world-famous, but it was pretty good. Sheila had forgotten to call, and when I arrived, a little after dinner (which was totally my fault, the day had gotten away from me), I was met at the back door by a shotgun with Mr. Kirch at the other end of it, requesting that I *state* my *business*. That was the worst example I can recall of Sheila and me dropping the ball on a story.

Fortunately, this guy at the register didn't have a gun pointed in my face. Unfortunately, he didn't look like he was in any hurry to grant me access to the golfers, either in the bar area or on the course.

"Sir…" I said.

"You can call me Bogey."

"*Bogey?*"

"Yeah, it's not my real name," he snorted. "It's just a name the fellas gave me. Real name's Henry Hollinger. I pretty much run the daily operations of the Golf Club. If you have any questions, they can go through me."

I nodded and fumbled in my purse, looking for my phone. "Do you mind if I record you while we talk?"

"How long's this whole rigamarole gonna take," he said, looking at an imaginary watch on his wrist and then staring those cold blue eyes back at me.

"I don't know," I stammered. "A few minutes, maybe a half an hour…if you don't mind."

"And how much are you payin' for this?" He folded his arm across his chest and rocked back and forth on his feet.

"Oh," I said, taken aback by the request. I'd never before had anyone I was interviewing ask how much they were going to be compensated for their time. "We don't pay you. We print a story in the paper which gives you some publicity and hopefully a little extra business for the Golf Club."

"Well," he mused, scratching his head as he thought things over. "I don't really know that we need any more business. Things here look pretty busy, don't they? I mean, we can only fit so many golfers on the course as it is."

I was befuddled. I'd been doing this newspaper thing for years, and never before had I ever had a single person turn down an article because it would bring more people to their business. And from where I was standing, it looked like the course emptied out in the afternoon.

The wheels in my head started turning, thinking of another angle I could take with this Bogey guy, who was staring me down like he expected me to just slink away and crawl beneath the rock I'd come out from.

"Ha, ha, ha," he stepped back and clapped his hands together. The sound was so loud, like that of a firecracker going off right in front of me. "The look on your face is priceless," he continued, bending over at the waist, disappearing from my view momentarily before coming back up and putting his hands on his hips.

He flashed a smile at me and extended his hand. "I'm just messing with ya!"

I tentatively reached my hand out and shook his. It was dry and rough.

"Sheila called me this morning and told me you were coming." He came out from behind the bar, walked over to the window, and held his hands to show me what I could clearly see…a nearly empty course. "Afternoons get pretty slow around here. Does it look like we're so busy here I could afford to turn away business?"

"Not really," I managed.

"I mean, don't get me wrong," he said, tugging up at his belt buckle, "we're not broke or anything. But more golfers is better than fewer golfers."

I nodded. And then attempted to get him back on track.

"So, you're up for an interview?"

"Oh, me?" He pointed at himself and shrugged his shoulders. "Heavens no. Sheila said you wanted to interview David Gardner. He's won the tournament four years in a row."

"That would be better," I said, hoping not to offend him.

"You don't have to make that look with your face," he replied. "You're not hurting my feelings by not wanting to talk to me. Truth be told, I don't really want to talk to you much, either."

He walked back over toward the register and grabbed a clipboard off the bar. He moved his finger up and down the first page and then flipped to the second page. Tapping his finger near the top of the second sheet, he exclaimed, "There he is."

Holding up a finger, he scooted behind the counter and grabbed a key that was attached to a big diamond-shaped piece of plastic. It had the number fifteen on it.

"You're going to take cart fifteen out there. Just put this in the —"

"I know how to drive a golf cart," I interrupted.

"Oh," he stood up straight as if no other woman had ever told him that she could do something he was explaining to her. "Well, in that case, David Gardner should be finishing up on hole thirteen now. Your best bet is to find the tee box for number fifteen and wait there for him."

I took the key from him and said, "Thank you for your help, Bogey. How will I know which one is David Gardner?"

"Well, for starters, he always golfs alone. And if you need more information, he's wearing a shirt that matches your clothes."

"Thank you for your help."

I turned to head out to the cart area, wondering where on earth the fifteenth-hole tee box was located.

"You'll want one of these," Bogey called. I turned around to see him holding something in his hand. "It's a scorecard. On the back is a map of the course." He walked over to me and pointed at a gray square on it. "You're here. You'll want to follow this path. Hole fifteen is here." He moved his finger along a line the width of a pencil point.

"Thanks again," I nodded. Then I took the score card out to find cart fifteen. Now that it had been explained to me, how difficult could finding David Gardner be?

4

———

A gentle breeze blew through my hair as I walked out of the Pro Shop.

Carts were lined in three neat rows, all facing the same direction, all numbered, not in order. My eyes scanned the first row of carts, finding the one I was looking for smack dab in the middle of everything.

I walked over to the cart and put the key in the ignition, turned it to the right, and was instantly greeted by a very loud buzzing sound.

Oh no, I thought, *I broke it!*

Quickly, I turned the key back to the left and removed it. The buzzing noise stopped.

"You need a little help there?" A man asked. He was backing his cart into the row on the end, about five carts away from mine, the same buzzing coming from his cart.

He appeared to be in his late forties, with a mostly slender build. His belly jutted out ever so slightly, stretching the fabric on his navy blue polo, giving a tip to the notion that he liked his beer after a hard day's work.

I smiled and laughed nervously. "I think, maybe, I do."

He hopped out of the cart he was in and walked over to mine. He was wearing a neon green baseball cap, but I could tell that he had a nice thick head of blond hair that, no doubt, matched his tanned skin and blue eyes nicely. "You see that black knob beneath the rim of the seat?" He pointed at the middle of the cart seat. I couldn't help but notice that his teeth were impeccable.

I looked down. Next to my knee was a big black thing tilted toward the left.

"Right now, your cart's in reverse. See that letter 'R' above the knob?"

I nodded that I did.

"Well, that needs to be pointed at the letter 'F'. That'll get you moving forward. Apparently, the last person who had your cart forgot to move that back before they left." He tipped his head toward the back of my cart, smiling. "And it looks like he may have had good reason."

I turned to see what he was looking at. In a black basket behind the seats was a clear plastic bag half filled with ice.

"I don't...." I stammered, "What's that?"

"Nothing much," the man said. "Just an empty plastic

bag full of ice where six beers used to be." He extended his hand out. "My name's Chester Frank."

I shook Chester's hand. "I'm Connie Cafe. I'm sure you could tell by now that this is not exactly my scene."

He took his hand back and tucked it away in the pocket of his shorts. "Well, I wasn't going to mention anything, but since you brought it up...."

We shared a laugh for a few seconds before he asked, "So, what does bring you here?"

"I'm writing an article for *The Coffee Creek Gazette* about this weekend's upcoming tournament. I'm just on my way out to see if I can snag an interview with David Gardner."

Chester nodded and folded his arms across his chest, rocking back on his heels. "Well, good luck with that." He turned and looked over both of his shoulders to make sure no one could hear him, then he leaned forward and said, "Just between you and me, he can be a real S.O.B."

"Well," I faltered, unsure what to say to that. "I will certainly keep that in mind."

"In fact," Chester moved forward, putting his foot up on the cart, "I'd have won that tournament last year if it wasn't for that dirty, good for nothin'...." His voice trailed, and he took his eyes off of me and started looking off somewhere into the trees. He took a few deep breaths and then removed his foot from the cart. "Anyway, I should probably let you go. I have no doubt you'll find out what a fantastic fella *Mr. God's Gift to Golf* is in no time. It was nice to meet you...."

"Connie," I offered, noticing that he was having trouble remembering my name.

"Connie," he snapped his fingers. "That's right. Sorry about that. Well, it was nice to meet you, Connie. Good luck with your interview." He pulled a small card from his back pocket and handed it to me. "If you find that David's not exactly the most interesting guy in the world, feel free to give me a call. This is my business card. That bottom number goes directly to my personal cell phone." He tapped the pocket of his shorts to show me just how close he kept his personal cell phone. "I own *Chester's High-End Jewelers* in town, and if that's not enough, I've been runner-up in the tournament you're reporting on for the last five years. Always a bridesmaid, I'm afraid. But still not too shabby."

He gave a half bow, backing away from the cart, and in a grand sweeping gesture, moved his arm and hand in the direction I was to drive.

"Thank you very much," I replied, though I was starting to lose patience at this point in the exchange. It was already after two O'clock, I hadn't eaten lunch, I hadn't interviewed anyone, and I had to have the article sent off to Sheila by five.

I put the key back in the cart's ignition and shifted the black knob into the 'F' position before putting my foot down on the gas pedal. The brake pedal popped up loudly, giving me a bit of a start. The cart lurched forward, which just about threw me out of the seat.

A few guys nearby had looked over to see who was creating all the commotion. I could feel my face flush red as they began to laugh.

It took me a moment to settle myself back into the seat. The next time I put my foot on the gas, it was done with a little more grace. I slowly drove past Chester, and the rest of them, down the cart path to find hole number fifteen.

I FOLLOWED the path as far as possible before running into a group of four golfers. They were teeing off on hole ten. I looked at the map and thought that it wasn't exactly the easiest set of directions to follow.

"You don't have any clubs," one of the golfers noticed. He was an older guy with thinning white hair and a gentle smile. "I'm guessing you're not here to golf."

"Correct." I flashed him a grin. "I'm on my way to hole fifteen. I have Bogey's permission, but, honestly, I'm having a terrible time figuring out this map."

"Not to worry," the man said. "Those maps are horrible." He pointed off to my left. "Just scoot right across those two holes there. It's okay to drive on the grass. You're not going to hurt anything. Just be sure to check for golfers before you cross. Getting hit in the head by a golf ball or getting yelled at by an angry foursome's no fun at all. When you get through that set of pines over there, you'll see a sign for the fifteenth hole. The tee box will be right there."

"Wonderful," I chirped. "Thank you so much for your help. You are, honestly, the kindest person I've run into out here."

"Well, you're very welcome," he said, bowing his head slightly. "Do you mind if I ask what you want to do on hole fifteen?"

"I'm interviewing David Gardner about the upcoming tournament this weekend."

"Good luck with that," the man huffed. "Take my advice, lady. Talk to someone else. You could do a lot better than that piece of work."

"A job's a job," I shrugged. "But thanks for the words of advice. I will tell you that you're not the first person who's told me that."

I gave a little wave and drove off in the direction he showed me, very careful to look in all directions for potentially angry golfers and their fast-moving golf balls.

A few tense moments later and I was perfectly positioned next to the tee box for hole fifteen.

Nobody else was there.

The sign had a number three on it. The scorecard said it was one hundred and eighty-three yards from the blue tees, which were the furthest back. Since David Gardner had won the tournament for a few years now, I figured this would be where he would be going to take his first shot on the hole.

I pressed down hard on the brake, snapping the parking lock into position so I wouldn't go rolling away. The last thing I needed was more cart issues.

My phone screen read 2:15. I'd taken a few minutes to get over here. My guess was that David Gardener would be finishing up the fourteenth hole in the next few minutes and be walking over to me before two-thirty. If I could talk to him for a few minutes and get a couple of good quotes, I was sure I could do a few internet searches about golf and get enough information to finish my five hundred words by five o'clock.

Lunch, on the other hand, was a different story. Today was shaping up to be a two-cup of coffee day, followed by dinner and bed. Not exactly what I would call ideal.

But it happened more than I cared to admit.

MY STOMACH WAS GROWLING.

I'd stolen a few glances at my phone and had taken to tapping my foot irritatedly against the black flooring of the golf cart.

Where is this guy? I thought to myself.

I'd heard from everyone else that I'd talked to leading up to this that he was rather unpleasant to be around. If he didn't come walking off that fourteenth green in the next two minutes, he'd be sharing *his* stories tomorrow about The Queen B that works for *The Gazette*.

My butt and back needed a break and a stretch. I stood up and got out of the cart, and walked up onto the tee box to see what this game was all about.

I'm sure I looked rather dumb taking practice swings with no club in my hand to speak of and imagining where my ball would end up.

In my mind, it seemed so easy to just stand here and hit a ball in the direction of the green. A little yellow flag waved at me. I also noticed how peaceful and quiet it was out here. The calm, quiet breeze rustled the leaves of a rather large tree that was set off to the right-hand side of the tee box.

A squirrel was perched up on one of the branches about halfway up. I stared in wonder and awe at how still he was, his furry tail standing straight up. His mouth was feverishly working on an acorn. *Even a squirrel gets to have lunch once in a while,* I mused. Unfortunately for him, the acorn slipped and dropped to the base of the tree with a thud.

I kept my eyes on the squirrel, wondering what his next move would be. My money was on him staying put and letting that acorn rest where it was. Much to my surprise, he popped down off the branch and skittered so quickly, he looked like he was flying to the bottom of the tree trunk.

Little did I know that this would not be the only surprise that came my way as a result of watching this furry little guy.

When he was on his way down, something off to the side caught my attention. I wasn't sure what it was at first. It was brightly colored, off toward the back of the tree, in a pond, I didn't even realize was there.

It was the same salmon color as my blazer and pants — and it was floating.

A rush of adrenaline met my empty stomach and forced me to wretch a dry heave. I felt lightheaded all of a sudden at the realization of what I was looking at.

Lying face down in the pond, behind the fifteenth-hole tee box, was the man I was sent to interview.

And according to my less-than-perfect calculations, David Gardner had been in there for a while.

5

David Gardner was the second dead person I'd ever seen in my life.

My father was the first.

But even when I'd seen my father, it had been at the funeral home, with friends and family nearby to hold me and tell me that things were going to be alright. He'd been made up expertly by the mortician and dressed in his finest suit. My father had looked so peaceful, like he was just taking a really long nap … in a casket … with everyone watching.

That hadn't been easy.

In fact, it had been the hardest thing I'd ever had to do in my life.

Until now.

This seemed harder.

I was all alone.

In an unfamiliar place.

With a man, I was supposed to meet, yet never got the chance.

The squirrel I'd admired just a moment ago for his cuteness and agility suddenly seemed creepy and cruel as he continued to gnaw away at his acorn less than twenty feet from a dead man.

The quiet and calm that I'd appreciated just a few moments earlier now seemed eerie and ominous. The leaves were rustling, but it wasn't the same noise it had been before.

At least not to me.

This wasn't exactly a situation I'd ever dreamt of finding myself in. I had, at times, thought about how I would handle an emergency. Would I be calm, cool, and collected in the face of it?

The answer, I now realize, is a resounding: No!

I don't know how long it took me to reach for my phone and call 9-1-1, but I know that it wasn't immediate.

I knelt there for a few minutes on top of the tee box. My eyes kept moving from the squirrel to the dead man to the rustling leaves. It was as if, at that moment, I'd completely forgotten about God and replaced Him with a different holy trinity altogether: The squirrel, the leaves, and the floating dead man - Amen.

I knew I hadn't. Even still, not a prayer came forth from my lips, no request for guidance or wisdom.

I chose to struggle.

On my own.

That's what I chose to do.

To anyone who was watching or the police officers who would eventually come upon the scene I'd called in about, it would look like I was deep in prayer. I was on my knees, hands folded in my lap, head hung deeply against my chest.

But that's not what I was doing.

I was trying to catch my breath, to get my bearings back in place, to figure out a way to stand up again and walk away from this nightmare.

A hand came down in front of my face after I didn't know how long. It was attached to an arm wearing a blue uniform. For the first time all day, I was truly grateful.

I didn't even know whose hand it was. I just knew that it was what I needed at that moment.

"Hey, Connie," a deep voice whispered to me. "It's time to get up. Take my hand…I'll help you."

THE HAND BELONGED to Officer Theodore Billings. I went to school with Theodore when we were kids. Back then, he was called *Teddy*. Now, he's just *Ted*.

He was a year or two older than me. I can't remember ever actually talking to him about anything when we were in school. Then, I went away to college and lost touch with most people. By the time I came back, a great deal of the people I'd gone to school with were in various stages of their careers, raising families, and far too busy to relive the old days.

Not that I was in any place to do that when I moved back after my father's death. That was a tough time; another time in my life when I'd felt helpless, a time when I needed the strong yet gentle hand of God to guide me through my troubles and help me get back on my feet again.

Officer Billings guided me gently down the side of the tee box and back into the golf cart, telling me, "It's okay," every step of the way. I followed, feeling like I was watching myself from outside of my body. "Just sit here for a few moments. I'll be over to ask you some questions shortly." His voice was gentle and calming.

I nodded and watched as he strode back up and over the tee box and back down the other side in the direction of David Gardner's body.

There were several police officers on the scene, along with an ambulance, just in case resuscitation was possible.

It wasn't.

Bogey had made his way over from the Pro Shop and was standing off to the side at a distance as the police had requested. Along with him were about a dozen other golfers who'd come out to see what was going on.

"Such a shame," I heard Bogey say to one of the onlookers. "He was such a good man."

"And a great golfer," one of the golfers replied, removing his hat and holding it over his heart as if he was mourning a fallen soldier.

Officer Billings walked over to the gathered group and pulled Bogey aside.

"Listen," I overheard him saying, "I hate to do this, but we're going to have to ask you to close the course for the rest of the day and possibly tomorrow while we conduct our investigation."

Bogey nodded his compliance. "I understand. Can you tell me one thing?"

"What's that?"

"Will we still be able to have the tournament on Saturday? I realize that sounds rather trite at this point in time, but, honestly, officer, it's a big money maker for us."

Officer Billings nodded. "You should be able to have the tournament. I can't promise anything at this point, but we're still a few days out. That should be enough time."

Bogey nodded again and thanked Billings.

Billings then walked over to me and said, "How ya doing, Connie?"

"I've had better days," I said emotionlessly.

"I bet. I'm really sorry that you had to see this today."

"Me too." I forced a little smile, hoping to keep the tears from welling up in my eyes. I failed. "I'm sorry," I said, wiping my eyes with the sleeve of my blazer. "I'm sure you have enough work to do without having to console some crying reporter."

He looked up over the tee box, craning his neck to get a good view of what was transpiring, before crouching down and holding my hand. "Those guys have it under control. I'm right where I need to be right now."

"Thank you," I said. "I appreciate all of this."

"Not a problem at all, Connie." He looked around to make sure no one was looking. "Between you and me, I'm the best officer we've got for this sort of thing." He gave me a wink and shot me a quick smile, the smell of peppermint gum mingled with his cologne. "You know, I'm the soft, sappy, and super sensitive guy on the force. Usually, it comes with a lot of ridicule, but today the other guys are quite thankful I'm here."

I smiled. I was in agreement with those other guys and very thankful that he was here, too.

It was getting on to about five O'clock. All of the golfers had left the course, including Bogey, while evidence was collected.

Officer Billings gave me his card and told me he'd be in touch in the next day or two, but if I needed anything or could remember anything that might help them figure out what happened, not to hesitate to call.

I took his card and slid it into my purse before getting into my car and heading home.

When I reached the front porch of the house, my

mother was at the top of the stairs, arms open, waiting to offer me a hug, a warm home-cooked meal, and a hot bath.

Numb.

That's how I felt.

And even though my mother had gone to great lengths to cook up a wonderful meal (roasted lemon herb chicken, rice pilaf, and fresh asparagus from Gustafson's Farm, with a beautiful semi-dry Riesling from Washington State), I don't remember tasting a bite of it.

I knew I'd eaten. I could feel the food in my stomach, and I could see that my plate and glass were empty where once they had been full.

But I didn't remember any of it.

"Would you like some tea?" My mother asked as she cleared the table and filled the old farmhouse sink with warm, sudsy water. "Perhaps, a nice cup of chamomile. Maybe a fun read and a bubble bath would help."

"No thanks," I said, staring vacantly across the kitchen. "I think I'm just going to head up to bed."

"Okay, honey." I could hear the defeat in her voice. I knew that she desperately wanted to help me through this, but I didn't know how to allow it. I didn't want to seem distant or cold, or dismissive, but I felt like I had no control over it.

I stood up and pushed my chair in. "I love you," I told my mother. "I'll see you in the morning."

"Love you too, pumpkin."

When I got to my room, I picked up my Bible and began searching for something, anything, that would help guide me through these feelings I was experiencing.

I had so many emotions going through my head and heart that I was having trouble unpacking them all.

What was I feeling?

Shock, you bet. David Gardner's floating body was the last thing in the world I'd expected to see when I left the house for work.

Sadness, yup. I hadn't heard many good things from anybody about David Gardner, but he was a child of God. Because of this, I know that he must've been important to someone, someone who is missing him.

Fear. In droves. I'd lived around Coffee Creek for all of my life, save a few years away at college. Nothing like this had ever happened here, so far as I knew. The small town that had been my home, a place I had thought of as peaceful and even boring at times, now suddenly felt so foreign. Would I ever be able to feel the same way about going to work, walking around Main Street with a cup of coffee, popping into shops, or reading books on one of the benches that overlook the creek?

I had to stop myself there. Maybe I'd read too many books. For all I knew, David Gardner's death was an acci-dent. Officer Billings hadn't said one way or another. Only that they were investigating it, and that they would be in contact shortly. But even that made it feel like David Gardner's death was suspicious and, therefore, possibly not an accident.

Take a deep breath, Connie, I chided myself. *Get a grip. Relax. Read your scripture, say a prayer, and get some sleep.*

Deep breath. Check.

Scripture. Check.

> *Do not worry about tomorrow, for tomorrow will worry about itself. Each day has enough trouble of its own.*
>
> *~Matthew 6:34*

Prayer: The Lord's Prayer. Check.

Get some sleep.

Not a chance.

6

My mother, dressed in a stunning Egyptian Blue dress that pulled off both modest and sultry, was standing near the coffee pot in the corner of the kitchen.

She was tapping her feet as per usual, waiting for the final drip of coffee to run through the filter and drop into the already very full pot.

My mug was sitting on the counter next to hers.

"I heard you tossing and turning all night long," she said, taking the pot off the burner and filling our cups to the brim. "I know what kind of a day it's going to be."

She winked as she handed me the mug.

"Yeah," I nodded. "Thanks."

"You want to talk about anything?" She offered.

I shook my head and brought the steaming mug of coffee up to my lips, my left hand wrapped around the hot edge of it.

"Not right now," I said after the first miraculous sip. "Sheila emailed and texted me this morning and wants to meet about something. I don't know what yet, but it must be urgent for her to send a text."

My mother looked concerned. "Are you sure it's a good idea for you to go to work today?"

"Sure it is," I said, trying to convince myself more than her. "Why wouldn't I go to work? It's not like I knew the guy."

Bobbing her bright red hair up and down, my mother said, "I know you didn't know him. But that's not the point, is it? Yesterday, you saw something horrible. Something few people ever have to experience. Don't you think a break would be acceptable? Maybe even necessary?"

I set my mug down and walked over to my mother, placing my hand on her shoulder. "Mom, I know you're concerned, but trust me when I tell you, I'm a big girl now. I can take care of myself. I know what happened yesterday was upsetting and difficult, but I'll be fine."

She closed her eyes and sighed. I gave her a kiss on her forehead before turning around and heading for the door.

"I love you, mom. I'll be fine. Trust me."

ABOUT HALFWAY TO *The Coffee Creek Gazette* offices, I was kicking myself for not taking my mother's advice. That old expression, *Mother Knows Best,* was ringing in my ears.

Although, that ringing could have been the fact that I was working on about twenty minutes of sleep and no caffeine.

I pulled into the parking lot of the *Gazette* a few minutes after nine and put the car in park.

Sheila didn't even wait for me to open the door before she bolted down the steps and into the parking lot. She was wearing her Tuesday outfit, which was a maroon dress with hideous orange flowers all over it. As usual, the shoulder pads were very pronounced. She had a run in her nude stockings, and watching her run across the stone drive was a sight to behold.

Honestly, I wished it could have lasted longer. And knowing now what she was about to ask of me, I wish it could have lasted long enough for me to throw the car into reverse and speed off before she had a chance to reach me.

But that stuff's all hindsight and twenty-twenty and all that jazz.

"Oh good, you're here," she huffed as she practically ripped the driver's side door off my car. "I was worried you weren't going to show today."

This was awkward.

I didn't know if I was supposed to just sit in my car

and listen to her ramble, or if I was supposed to slide out
of my car and stand in the parking lot next to her…and
listen to her ramble.

Sliding out seemed like the closest thing to professional
in this situation, so that's what I did.

And if Sheila's run across the parking lot, her tremen-
dously hideous Tuesday outfit, and her out-of-breath
greeting weren't unsettling enough, my attempting to slide
out past her without our bosoms touching was the most
uncomfortable part of the entire scene. I nearly ended up
falling on my backside in the process.

It took me a moment to regain my balance and stand
up straight in front of her. Much to my surprise, she was
still going strong, and I hadn't heard a word she'd said.

"Hold on," I said, putting my hand up to block her
face. I know this wasn't the best way to ask my boss to
back up and start over, but on little sleep and a sip of
coffee, it was the best I could muster.

Through her makeup, I could make out an expression
of surprise and disappointment.

But she did stop talking.

For a moment.

"I'm sorry," I said, bringing my hand back down to my
side. "It's just, well, I haven't had a lot of sleep, and my
coffee intake for the day is next to nothing. Would you
mind terribly if I asked you to start from the beginning
and catch me up to speed slowly?"

"Of course," she said, flashing me her all too familiar fake smile, and taking a deep breath to compose herself. "I was saying, that we need to move fast on this one. We've got a real scoop here! This story could put *The Coffee Creek Gazette* on the map!"

I blinked a few times and stared at her, dumbfounded. There was no way she was referring to David Gardner's death at the golf course as an opportunity for our small-town paper to gain notoriety and gather some momentum, was she?

The answer to that question was, yes, she was.

"Think about it, Connie," she continued, her mascara starting to run down her rosy cheeks as the sun and her impromptu workout session caught up with her. "How amazing would it be if our own reporter, the reporter who found the body, at that, was the same person to solve this murder?"

"Murder?" I'd thought about the possibility that David Gardner had been murdered last night before bed, but those were my private thoughts. The police hadn't announced anything yet, so far as I was aware. "I thought his death was still under investigation. Isn't it a little early for *The Gazette* to announce to the world that it was a homicide?"

"Well, you're the one to find out all those goodies, and then write them down and send them to me. Your stories will be on the front page for weeks to come, maybe months, if you do a good job." She smiled, her lipstick-stained teeth in full view of anyone within a twenty-mile radius. "What do ya say?"

"No. Not in a million years would I ever dream of trying to capitalize on a man's untimely death. That's just wrong, plain and simple."

I couldn't believe what Sheila was doing. She'd always seemed like such a good person, a little frazzled and scatterbrained, sure, but never slimy. But this. This was slimy.

"Suit yourself," she huffed and turned on her heels to go back into the office.

"Jeff!" She called.

Jeff opened the door quickly like he'd been standing there, waiting to see what my answer was going to be. And as soon as he heard that I wasn't willing to go along with Sheila's grand plan, he was there, ready to pounce, willing and able.

"Yes, Sheila," he replied, flashing me a dirty little smirk from his rickety old perch of power.

"Come inside, Jeffrey. We are going to talk about a way that you can get on the front page of the paper for the foreseeable future."

She opened the door and allowed Jeff Toobin to slink in before she turned to me. "Connie, you'll be covering Jeff's expose on the village sanitation department for the next two weeks." She looked my outfit up and down. I was wearing a long, flowing dress, white with red polka dots. It was so comfy on days like this, plus it looked great. "You'll want to wear pants and a shirt for that assignment. Nothing fancy. It'll just get ruined."

Then she turned and let the door slam behind her.

Well, I thought to myself, *that could have gone better.*

7

I had no idea what to expect when I drove over to the coffee shop.

Actually, yes, I did.

I knew it was going to be a mess. I knew I was going to have to clean it up. I knew Reba was going to be upset with me for not being there during the morning rush, even though I'm not on the schedule until after the rush goes through.

I knew all of that was coming my way. What I didn't know was how I was going to react to it. I was trying to get my bearings and trying to avoid going full-on woe is me.

Much to my surprise, when I opened the door to the shop, Reba was standing there in her green apron, her piercing blue eyes staring at me consolingly. She held out a large paper cup with a cardboard ring that had my name written on it in big permanent marker letters.

"I just got off the phone with your mother. She said you'd need this today."

"Wait! What? How were you on the phone with my mother? Did you call her? Do you even know her number? Do you even know my mother? How much have you heard?"

Reba nodded and smiled, and pushed the coffee forward. "Your mother was right. You are in rough shape this morning. Have a few sips of this, and let's dull the edge of that razor, shall we."

I grabbed the coffee and took a few sips as I walked over to the counter. My apron was already on the corner and folded neatly, just waiting for me to put it on. I glanced behind the counter, and much to my surprise, it was sparkling.

Everything had been cleaned up. The cups were stacked neatly, the trash had been emptied, the blenders were clean and in place, three full pots of coffee awaited the mid-morning rush, and three more were empty with coffee makers loaded just in case we needed them.

"Who are you?" I turned and stared at Reba. "And what have you done with the woman I work with?"

Reba chuckled and took her place behind the register, leaning against the back counter.

"Let's start at the beginning," she began. "Your mother called here early this morning before all the morning yahoos came in expecting their daily dose. She said you'd had a really rough night. That's really all she said. Well, that and that you didn't have more than a sip of coffee this morning."

"That's all she said?" I was concerned that my mother may have spilled the beans about why my night was so rough. And honestly, I didn't want to get into it right at the moment.

"Yup," Reba said, "that's all she said. Now, if you want to say more about things, the counselor is in." She popped herself up onto the counter, using it like a chair. Something the boss would have hated if he were around.

Thankfully, for Reba, he liked to spend as much time as possible in the back office of the shop, away from people.

On days like this, I thought, *that might just be the best place to be.*

I MANAGED to make it through my shift at the coffee shop without Reba asking about too much.

That didn't mean it was a nice, easy-going shift, though. She kept staring at me, those blue eyes boring a hole straight down into my soul. She knew I had a secret and that I wasn't going to tell her what it was. And that was making her crazy.

It felt awful to know I was letting Reba down. Especially after all that she had done for me this morning to help get me back on my feet.

Before I left the shop, I thanked her for her efforts and told her that I really wanted to tell her what was on my mind but just couldn't. "I'll let you know as soon as I feel like I can."

All she did was put her hands on her hips and give me a, *yeah, right,* look as I took off my apron and headed for my car.

The sun was high in the sky, and it was much warmer than usual for a late May day. This spring was unusually warm.

My mind was shifting towards my afternoon assignment of interviewing the *Coffee Creek Sanitation Department* people.

That thought, coupled with the heat of the day and the knowledge of how much that was going to affect the smell of things this afternoon, made it easier for me to put Reba in the back of my mind for the time being.

I'd eventually tell her everything she thought she needed to know.

Right now, I was going somewhere else.

And there wasn't a clothespin in Coffee Creek big enough to save me.

Dear God,

It's me, Connie. Right now, I'm on the back of a garbage truck. Though, they don't really call them garbage trucks. They're called 'Motorized Sanitation Receptacles' or 'Refuse Collection Vehicles.'

Either way, I'm on the back of one right now, wondering why I didn't listen to my mother when she suggested that I stay home this morning. I am also praying that I make it home without throwing up in front of Derek Snider. He's the rough and tumble looking guy with too much facial hair and not enough shirt, who keeps looking at me every time we hit a bump, or a big gust of wind comes blowing my way. I can't tell if he's hoping to see something or if he has general concern for my safety.

I can't bring myself to look at him, O' Lord. And it's not because I'm too good or anything like that. I couldn't possibly be that way. It goes against the very tenants of my faith and everything You have taught me to be. Rather, I can't look at him because I'm afraid I'm going to vomit, and I would just die if any of it were to get on that poor man.

Dear Lord, his job is hard enough as it is. This much I now understand. And it is because of this that I will forever and always be sure to separate my recyclables properly and make sure that I don't overstuff the garbage bags anymore.

Also, Lord, I pray for Marty Dennings, who seems to take better care of his hygiene than Derek. I can't say I blame either of them for their approach, for Marty rides up front every day, which is significantly better than holding onto the back of the truck like Derek. I pray that he can guide us to safety so that I may get back into my car and drive home. Once home, I promise to burn this dress and take the longest, hottest shower I've ever taken before in my life.

After that, I will enjoy a nice dinner with my mother. I will talk to her about important things in my life, and I will not shield her from the pain and anguish I've been trying to hide. I will then take the advice I should've taken this morning and stay home from work for the remainder of the week to help me sort through everything. I now realize how wrong I was and how my stubbornness in the face of turmoil has rendered me less than helpful to anyone.

Thank you, Lord, for helping me see this. I wish it would have been a little more subtle than it was, but I know you work in mysterious ways. It's our job to clear our minds of clutter to accept you in the best way we possibly can. And the smell wafting out of this moving garbage can has truly cleared my mind and helped me to see the error of my ways.

Thank you, Lord, for making it crystal clear to me what the right and proper directions are for this child of yours. I am forever indebted to you.

In your holy name, I pray,
AMEN

IN TYPICAL FASHION, my mother had outdone herself. She prepared medium-rare New York strip with melted Roquefort and garlic butter, gently set on top of a platform of the most amazing steamed asparagus (steamed in garlic and sauvignon blanc from New Zealand). Roasted potatoes with Thyme and Rosemary, along with a full-bodied Chilean Malbec, tied everything together.

Unlike the night before, I enjoyed and savored every bite.

"You were right," I said, coating my mouth with wine, forever in awe of how the steak, cheese, and butter transformed into something truly transcendent with the addition of well-fermented and oak-aged grapes.

Absolutely, something to behold. Dare I say, better than coffee.

"How so?" My mother leaned forward, a devilish grin on her face. "Go ahead, honey. Tell me how amazing I am."

I smiled as the last of my sip of wine rushed down my throat. "I should have taken a day off of work. I wasn't ready to go back today."

My mother nodded. "Tell me more, sweetie."

"There's not much to tell, really," I said. "I mean, I spent the afternoon on the back of a garbage truck, trying not to vomit on Derek Snider and talking to God, hoping he would show me the way."

It was hard to look at my mother. She was listening so intently, but the smile that had formed on her face was going from ear to ear.

"Yeah," I surrendered. "It does sound pretty funny when I put it that way."

"You're darn right it's funny," she burst out laughing.

I followed suit, unable to control myself. I'd been holding on to such strong emotions, trying to figure everything out, that it was like someone or something hit the release valve on the pressure cooker, and the only thing I could do to blow out the steam was laugh uncontrollably.

The good time was short-lived, however.

My phone rang. I checked my watch to see who was calling me.

"Mom, I've gotta take this." My mother's eyes went from jovial to concerned in record time. She knew I would never take a phone call during dinner unless it was important. Her eyes were begging me to tell her who was calling. "It's the police station."

"Go ahead, answer it," she nodded.

I reached for my phone, fumbling with it as it slid free from the all-too-tight pockets in my jeans.

"Hello," I said. My voice was shaky as I answered. "This is she."

My mother leaned forward, trying to hear what the person on the other end of the call was saying to her baby.

"I see … Yes, I will absolutely stop by first thing tomorrow morning … No problem … Okay, you too … Thanks."

I hung up and set the phone down on the kitchen table next to my half-full glass of wine.

"Honey, you look as white as a sheet. Are you okay?"

"I think so," I nodded. But I didn't know for sure. I had been expecting this call to come. Officer Billings told me it would come eventually. But still, the idea of having to go to the *Coffee Creek Police Station* and discuss my role in discovering the body of David Gardner wigged me out more than a little. "I have to go to the station tomorrow and answer some questions for them."

"I'm sure it's nothing," my mother assured me. "Just routine procedures. Dotting T's and crossings I's, I'm sure. Nothing to worry about." She raised her glass of wine in the air and said, "Now, what do you say we finish this wonderful meal, turn on one of those cheesy Hallmark movies you love so much and enjoy the rest of the evening?"

"That sounds good," I agreed, raising my glass and clinking it with my mother's before we both downed the entirety of our remaining wine.

"Let's clean up this mess and enjoy the rest of that wine with our movie," she winked and pointed to two mostly full bottles that were open on the counter.

And that's exactly what we did.

8

Walking into the police station seemed oddly familiar, and yet completely surreal.

I had walked up to this same single-story, red-bricked building, as a child of five or six, with my mother. I remember she had a big plate of homemade chocolate chip and peanut butter cookies. She'd piled them high on the platter and covered them tightly with plastic wrap.

We were bringing the officers cookies because they had helped my father out with something important, and my mother thought this was the best way to thank them.

I never did find out what they helped my father with, but I will never forget the happy faces and appreciation they shared for my mother's baking.

That was a happy memory that I'd carried with me for a long time.

Many years later, standing outside the station, staring at my much older reflection in the glass doors, I was apprehensive to open those doors and go inside. I was nervous that it would sully my happy memory of days gone by.

But I was a grown woman, not a little child. Time to *put away childish things*.

I took a deep, calming breath in, and whispered to myself, "Thy will be done, Lord. Thy will be done."

Then I grabbed the door and entered.

Much to my surprise, the police station hadn't changed much at all, based on what I could remember. It was almost exactly the same. White tile flooring, that had yellowed slightly after years of wear and tear. There were a few black scuff marks on it from where people failed to pick up their feet when they walked. Pale fluorescent lights bounced off of the eggshell-colored walls. The walls were adorned with headshots of prominent officers in their uniforms and caps, looking strong and brave, all in the same plain wooden frames.

The desks in the office matched the frames on the wall, as did the receptionist's desk upon entering.

Being a small town where nothing ever really happened, the *Coffee Creek Police Station* didn't have a receptionist.

When I walked in, the desk was empty. I stood silently, waiting for someone to notice that I had arrived.

It wasn't long, maybe a minute or two, and a young officer named Donald West walked over to the desk and sat down. He straightened a clipboard that was sitting there and picked up a pen.

Donald was new to the force, and I'd seen him around town a few times. I didn't know him well, but from what I could gather he seemed nice enough.

"Welcome to the *Coffee Creek Police Station*, what can I help you with?"

"Yes," I replied, clearing my throat. "I'm Connie Cafe. I was called last night about answering some questions regarding…." My voice trailed as I tried to find the correct words to describe what I was there to discuss.

"Ma'am," Donald nodded, bringing his voice down to a whisper. "I know why you're here. You're going to be talking to Officer Billings. I'll let him know you've arrived. Be back in a sec."

A sigh of relief flew out of me at not having to say the words 'dead body'.

He left the desk and went around a corner. Less than a minute passed, and Donald came back, Officer Billings walking tall, with purpose, behind him.

"Connie, thanks so much for coming," Officer Billings said as he came around the front desk to shake my hand. "Why don't you follow me and we'll try to get this done and over with as quickly as possible, so you can be on your way."

"Thank you," I nodded, and followed him around the corner, to a short hallway with two small offices. His was on the right.

It was a very tiny office, painted green with dark grey carpeting. He had a desk with a small monitor, keyboard, and mouse on top of it. To the side of the desk was a small, two-door filing cabinet, and a printer was sitting on a table, tucked away in the corner opposite the filing cabinet.

Officer Billings closed the door behind us and motioned me to sit in one of the two chairs facing his desk.

I obliged, and he walked around to the other side, shimmying his way between the file cabinet and the printer table. He sat in a small office chair, and there was a tiny window behind him, where the field that was located behind the building could be seen.

A man with long white hair, matted down by a green ball cap, wearing a t-shirt and a pair of faded blue overalls was on a big green lawn mower. He could be seen every so often as he went back and forth past the window.

"Sorry about the noise," Officer Billings smiled. "Today's lawn mowing day here at the station. Do you know Nigel Grundle?"

I nodded that I did, but struggled to find my voice. I looked down at my hands, noticing that my knuckles were white from gripping the top of my purse so tightly. I also noticed that if I moved my hands, sweat imprints would be left behind. I decided to keep them where they were. I crossed my legs at the ankle and sat up straight, my back not touching the chair at all.

"Yeah," Officer Billings said, perhaps trying to put me at ease. "Mr. Grundle's a good guy. Did you know he's been mowing the lawn out there since we were kids? Amazing," he said, shaking his head. "I can't imagine doing anything for that long."

"I know what you mean," I said, finding my voice, faint as it was.

"Anyway," he continued, opening his file cabinet and pulling out a file from the front. He opened it wide across his desk. "You're here to answer some questions about David Gardner. Can you go ahead and tell me what you were doing at the golf course?"

"I was doing a story for *The Gazette*," I managed. "We were doing a piece about the tournament in a few days."

"And what was the piece going to be about, specifically?" He had grabbed a pen and was starting to write things down on a sheet of paper.

"I'm not really sure, exactly. My editor, Sheila Robinson, sent me over to interview David Gardner. After that, I wasn't really sure what I was going to write."

"Interesting," he nodded. "Do you approach all of your stories like that?"

"Like what?"

"Not really knowing what you're going to write?"

I shifted uncomfortably in my seat, gripping my purse even tighter, which I hadn't even thought was possible prior to this moment. Talking about dead bodies was uncomfortable enough without bringing my writing process into the mix. I absolutely hate talking about my writing.

Officer Billings noticed my discomfort and began to smooth things over. "I'm asking because I've read your articles for years. I think you're a very talented writer, and I always thought you'd have a clear plan for what you wanted to write. At least, that's how it comes off to me. But hearing that you don't know ahead of time, makes your writing even more impressive."

He leaned back in his chair, the light catching his pale blue eyes. For the first time, I noticed how gentle they were, and I loosened my grip on my purse and set it down on the floor in front of me.

"Thank you," I blushed.

"You're welcome. So, you were going to interview David Gardner because he was last year's winner, and you were just going to see what he had to say and then write up a story for *The Gazette*?"

"That's correct."

"How did you know that he was going to be at hole fifteen?"

"The man at the Pro Shop…Bogey…told me if I drove out there, I'd be able to catch him. He gave me a map and said Mr. Gardner would be heading that way soon."

"And when you got there?"

"He was nowhere to be found. I waited in the cart for a while. But he didn't come."

"And then you found him in the water hazard?" Officer Billings said, clicking the top of the pen in and out. "How did that come about?"

I swallowed hard, not wanting to have to relive that part of the experience. "I was growing hungry and impatient. I'd been waiting there for about half an hour. So, I decided to get out and take a look around. And that's when I found him."

"And you called 9-1-1 right away?"

What kind of question was that? Why would he ask me that?

"Actually," I began, rubbing my hands on my pants. "It was a few minutes. I was in shock and didn't know what I was supposed to do." Realizing how bad that sounded, I backpedaled and tried to explain my slow response. "I had never seen a dead body before, except for my father at his funeral. It took me a few minutes to believe what I was seeing. As soon as I came to my senses, I called, and then you all showed up. Can I ask why you're asking me that question?"

"You can." Officer Billings put the pen down on his desk and sat up straight, clasping his hands together on top of his file. Suddenly, his comforting pale blue eyes didn't seem so comforting anymore.

"We believe David Gardner's death was a homicide. The cause of death was drowning. However, he had been struck in the back of the head and neck with what appeared to be a very thin stick or pole of some sort, which caused a significant amount of bruising. We haven't found the weapon yet."

I could feel the color drain from my face as he was telling me these things. The realization that I had missed witnessing a murder by a handful of minutes made me nauseous. But that wasn't the worst part of what Officer Billings had to say.

"Unfortunately, Connie, you were the one that found David Gardner. You were alone when you found him. The timeline from the time you arrived at the fifteenth hole and the time you called for assistance is substantial."

"So what are you trying to say?"

"I'm not trying to say anything." He shifted uneasily in his chair. "But it is my duty to let you know that based on the information we've collected so far, and based on the fact that David Gardner was alone at the time of his death, and you were the only one there with the body for a significant period of time, you are officially a suspect in the murder of David Gardner."

Murder?

Suspect?

Me?

How?

I felt hot and dizzy as a surge of adrenaline rushed

through my body. There were not enough prayers or deep breaths to calm me down.

"I'm a *suspect* in a murder investigation?"

"Officially, yes," Officer Billings nodded.

"What do you mean 'officially, yes'? You don't really believe that I did it, do you?"

I stared at him, and those beautiful blue eyes that just a few minutes ago had put me so at ease. They now looked back at me, and I didn't know what to think. What was going on behind those blue eyes? Was he looking at me like a criminal? Was he in fear for his life, sitting across from me at this moment? Did he have his hand on his gun beneath his desk? Was he just waiting for me to pull something out of my purse so he could take me down and wrap this investigation up?

"No," he said, raising his hands and pushing the air in the room down in an effort to de-escalate the situation. "No, I don't think you did it. But it's my job and my duty to let you know that you're someone we're looking at as a possible suspect. There's still a lot of work to be done. And one of the things I'm going to be working on is a way to prove that you didn't do it, so we can officially rule you out. But right now, unfortunate as it may be, you are a suspect."

I stood up and grabbed my purse. "Are we finished here? Am I allowed to go home? Or are you going to arrest me?"

"We are not going to arrest you," he replied. "And we

probably won't have to. You're free to go when you wish. Thank you for coming in."

I turned and walked toward the door of his office without saying a word.

He sidestepped his way around his desk and tried to grab the door handle for me, but I was already there.

I pulled the door open and took a few steps out into the hallway, noticing how loud my shoes were on the tile floor. I reached the end of the hallway and turned back to see him looking helpless, and defeated, leaning against the door jamb.

"I didn't do it," I proclaimed.

He nodded, a dejected look on his face, his hands in his pockets, looking like a helpless child being scolded by his mother.

I turned on my heel and walked through the station and out to my car without saying another word or looking anyone in the eyes.

As I arrived at my car, it was clear that I had to find out who killed David Gardner. It was officially a murder, and I was going to get to the bottom of it.

And not for Sheila Robinson, or *The Coffee Creek Gazette*.

No, I was going to find out who it was for me.

This was personal now.

9

"I don't know, honey," my mother said, gingerly taking a sip of iced tea. She'd just finished up with an appointment at the salon. Her lips were bright pink, her hair was bright orange, and her eyebrows and top lip were adorned with a red hue from where the wax had done its job.

We were sitting on the front porch of the house, overlooking the yard and country road. Cars were whipping by, paying no attention to us whatsoever.

"If I were you," she said, "I'd stay out of it and let the police do their work. I've been around long enough to know that this is just procedural stuff. Nobody in that town, or in that station, thinks for a second that you could possibly do something like that."

I stared blankly out across the road, watching the tall grass blow back and forth in the steady breeze. If it had been ten degrees cooler, it would have made for a very cool day. But as it was, the breeze made sitting on the front porch comfortable.

"I don't know, mom," I shook my head. "It just doesn't seem possible that I would be a suspect for anything, let alone someone's murder."

"Just give it a few days, Connie. They'll do some more digging, the way they do, and you'll be free and clear."

I heard what she was saying, heard it loud and clear. But I didn't agree with it, and I had no intention of taking her advice on this one.

I knew I was innocent, and if I had to give the police a hand in proving it, then that's exactly what I intended to do.

AFTER DINNER, I took a hot shower and cleared my head with a little prayer and meditation.

I pulled out one of my yellow legal pads and started flipping to a blank page. On my way to the blank one, I read a few of the pages I'd already written. They were full of ideas for my someday coffee shop. Ways to arrange the tables and chairs, how the serving bar would be situated, and what types of items would be on the menu. After all, it was going to be a coffee shop, not a restaurant. But food and coffee go together, so there had to be something. Most of the items were baked goods: tarts, strudels, cookies, pies, quiches, and things of that nature.

Most of the pages were lists of different types of coffee I'd considered stocking. There were so many sources of coffee, and so many different roasters, all doing great things. Eventually, I would like to get to a point where I could roast my own beans, and create my own blends — but not to start. To start, I would take it slow and steady, and make sure that I ordered the best coffee possible. I wanted my patrons to feel like they couldn't make coffee that good at home, and the ambiance of my shop would be like nothing they could get anywhere else.

All of these thoughts and dreams that I'd spent countless hours fixating and obsessing about, and they could all be gone because someone thought I might have killed the best golfer in town.

Once I found a blank page, I began scribbling down what I knew so far, as well as any questions I might have had about who David Gardner was, and who might possibly want to see him dead.

So far, I knew that he was pretty well hated among the golfing community. They respected him as a golfer, but everyone I talked to said he was a rotten human being. So sad, but so important.

I jotted down a note: *Get the list of players that were on the course when David died.*

I knew that he had died in the water hazard on the

fifteenth hole before I arrived. I also knew that he had been in the water for at least a half hour before I discovered him.

That was all that I knew for sure, or at least all I could think of after a few nights of sketchy sleep and a day when I was implicated as a suspect in a murder.

After this, I put my focus on the questions I had moving forward. For one, did David Gardner have a wife? And if he was married, would it be helpful to find her and attempt to have a conversation about what had happened?

Would Bogey be willing to help me out? Would he give me the list of golfers who were on the course during that time? Did they even keep that sort of thing? I thought I'd seen a sign-in sheet when I was talking to him at the bar, but that was a few days ago, and a lot had happened since then, so, I couldn't be sure.

A follow-up visit with Chester Frank. He had so many awful things to say about David Gardner and seemed so arrogant about his high-end jewelry shop in town. Plus, he stood to gain the most on the golf course by getting rid of David Gardner. What had he said? 'Always a bridesmaid', or something like that. What did that even mean? Do all guys say that? Or is it just arrogant jerks trying to talk tough to reporters?

Yeah, I'd have to talk to him, too.

The first thing the next morning, I was going to enjoy a few hot cups of coffee with my mother, if I could. And then *The Coffee Creek Golf Club* would be my destination.

That seemed like as good a place as any to start.

The scene of the crime.

10

"You're up early," my mother remarked as she headed to the shower in her fluffy, yellow bathrobe. If she were a little taller, she would have looked like a red-headed Big Bird.

"Yeah," I said, trying to avoid telling her where I was going. "I'm just feeling like I need to get out there and get some of that nice fresh air."

"Mmmhmmm," she said, shooting me a sideways glance.

She wasn't buying it. Not that I had sold it all that convincingly.

"I'm going to go fire up the coffee," I smiled, and backed away slowly before turning and heading down the long hallway to the stairs.

"Honey, do me a favor."

I stopped dead in my tracks, about five steps down. Somehow, I just knew that she was going to go on some long, motherly diatribe about how the police were going to sort things out, and everything was going to work out just fine, and I had absolutely nothing to worry about, and I should just stay out of it already because it's dangerous and inviting trouble isn't what I should be doing with my life.

But instead, she said, "Make the coffee strong. I have a feeling you're going to need your energy today." She winked at me and tucked herself into the bathroom before closing the door.

I smiled and shook my head. She knew and she wasn't going to try to stop me.

It wasn't like anything was going to stop me from trying to figure this thing out anyway, but knowing I had my mother's blessing certainly made it a little easier.

I ARRIVED at *The Coffee Creek Golf Club* around eight, after a wonderful breakfast with my mother…and multiple cups of coffee.

It was shocking that no one was out on the course. It was like the place was completely closed to the public. There was one other car in the parking lot, and I had a feeling I knew who that belonged to.

Walking into the Pro Shop, I found Bogey at the bar. He already had a glass of beer in his hand.

"What do you want?" he barked, setting his glass down a little harder than I think he meant. Although, he did seem pretty angry. So maybe it was exactly as hard as he'd meant.

"Well, good morning to you, too," I smiled, trying to break through the tension. Stepping up to the bar I said, "Bogey, I was wondering if you would be willing to let me go back out on the course in a cart this morning?"

"What are you gonna do? Haven't you messed up enough around here?" He slurred, extending both arms out toward the floor-to-ceiling windows that overlooked the eighth hole. "This course should be full this time of day. But not anymore. The cops shut us down for two days and guys went home to their wives and talked about how one of the guys got murdered here on the course, and all of a sudden nobody wants to golf."

"I'm so sorry, Bogey," I said. "But you have to believe me when I tell you that I had nothing to do with what happened to David Gardner, honest."

"You know how it looks, don't ya? You were all alone out there with him. At first, I wouldn't have believed it, a little thing like you overpowering a big man like David, but then the cops come in here yesterday and tell me that it's been confirmed a murder. You were the only one out there. Your own paper's running articles about you now."

He held up the most recent issue of *The Gazette*. I

almost threw up when I saw my picture on the front page with the title, 'Murderer, or Just in the Wrong Place at the Wrong Time?'

I grabbed the paper from his hand.

"I can't believe this." I held it up to him and pointed at the words that were printed above a rather horrible picture of me. "You don't believe this drivel, do you? They're mad at me over there at *The Gazette* because I refused to write stories like this. They're trying to get back at me for telling them no."

"I don't know." Bogey picked up his beer and took a healthy swig. "It says right in there that the police have already named you as a possible suspect. You know what else it says in that article?"

"No," I huffed. "What else does it say in that article?"

"It says right there, paragraph five, if I'm not mistaken, that you are the *only* suspect at the moment."

"Oh, for crying out loud. You don't actually believe that nonsense do you?" I stepped back a few feet so he could get a good look at the five foot four, hundred and ten-pound spectacle that is me. "Look at this!" I moved my hands from shoulders to knees and back again. "You don't really think that this could possibly do anything like what they're saying I supposedly did, do you?

"I don't know, ma'am."

"Connie," I said. "Call me, Connie."

"Ma'am, if you're a murderer, I don't really feel comfortable calling you much of anything."

I sighed.

"Well, it appears as though you already have your mind made up, don't you?"

He stood there silently, gawking at me.

"Your silence is speaking volumes," I said, backing away. "I'm smart enough to know that you're not going to give me a cart, so I'm just going to leave now so I don't make you any more uncomfortable."

I turned and walked out of the Pro Shop and out to my car.

Bogey didn't try to stop me.

My FIRST EFFORT at being a detective had failed, but that wasn't enough to stop me from doing what I needed to do.

I knew that if I just drove up the road a piece, I could catch the back side of the golf course on a side road heading out of town.

It wouldn't be ideal, but I could get out of my car and walk over to the fifteenth hole. I was pretty sure I remembered seeing the road from the tee box while I was checking emails on my phone a few days earlier.

Being a quiet road, I wouldn't have to worry about too many people seeing me.

Pulling out of the parking lot, I turned left and drove up the road about a quarter mile past the front nine of the course, and took a left onto County Route 37, which took you out away from Coffee Creek in the opposite direction from where mom and I live.

There were a few small houses on the corner of the road, and then nothing but high grass and dandelions.

I was about a third of a mile down the road when I found a place to pull over. Looking out at the back half of the golf course, I was hopeful that I could get over to the fifteenth hole in a few minutes without anyone seeing me. It would just require a quick jaunt through about twenty feet of field, and then I'd be in, so to speak.

Once I had gone through the field grass, I was on the course and in full-on stealth mode, hiding behind trees, ducking under signs, and cowering next to little plastic trash barrels that had far too many crushed cans, which wreaked of stale beer.

Yuck!

A few minutes after I left my car, I was standing next to the fifteenth-hole tee box, overlooking the water hazard where David Gardner had met his maker.

The first thing I noticed, which I hadn't on the day in question, was that this water hazard was incredibly shallow.

The police had been pretty thorough the other day and had spent several hours the day after the death, looking over the course for clues. But there was always a chance that they might have missed something.

"What are you doing here?"

My thoughts were interrupted by a voice I knew all too

well.

Jeff Toobin was walking over the tee box with a camera draped around his neck, a notepad and pen in his hands, and a smug smirk to boot.

"Oh, this is rich," he smiled. He placed the pen and notebook in his shirt pocket, and before I knew what he was doing, he grabbed his camera, pointed it in my direction, and pressed the button. A bright flash when off.

When my eyes came to, the camera was hanging down at his navel again.

"*What are you doing?*" I bellowed. I was beyond frustrated, and I'm sorry to say that I didn't feel the Holy Spirit moving through me as I stared at Jeff Toobin.

I hadn't murdered David Gardner, but if Jeff Toobin had gone missing at that moment, one wouldn't be so sure that it wasn't me who'd done it.

"I'm just doing my job," he grinned, putting his hands on his hips and puffing out his chest in some lame imitation of a superhero. "The better question, which, if I remember correctly, is one I already asked, is what are *you* doing here?"

"Just leave me alone," I said, turning away from him and back to my search for…anything.

"You've got some nerve," he said, not taking the hint and following me like a lap dog. "You know you could have done what you're doing now, and gotten paid for it. All you had to do was say yes to Sheila when she asked you."

"You don't listen very well." I continued walking away from him, less for myself, but more so I didn't turn around and smack him.

"Perhaps not, or perhaps so."

Oh great, I thought to myself. *Now, I'm going to get the all-too-familiar treat of Jeff Toobin waxing philosophically.* It was almost too much to bear. The Lord was putting me through a test today, for sure. And believe you me, He and I were going to have words about it later.

"Listening," Jeff kept on going, "is all dependent upon the person you're working for. You see, I don't work for you. But I do work for Sheila. Sheila told me to come out and get the scoop. In this case, you're the scoop. You are telling me to leave you alone. But you're not paying me. Sheila is. Thus, I listen to Sheila."

I stopped walking and turned around just in time to see Jeff coming up from his bow. *He actually bowed.* Like a performer, on a stage, after a great performance.

"What do you want? An interview with me? Well, you can forget that after what you wrote about me yesterday!"

"Would you be referring to the article where I stated only the facts in relating that you were the primary suspect in this murder investigation?"

"That would be the one," I snarled.

"Boy, are you testy." Jeff backed away, his hands raised above his head, mocking me. "Thankfully, we both know that you're not capable of something like that. What with your size, and your love of God. You wouldn't hurt a fly."

"Why did you write that about me then?" I asked. "It was completely horrible what you put in the paper. As if it wasn't bad enough before, the whole town of Coffee Creek is going to think I'm a murderer."

"First of all, nobody thinks you're a murderer."

"Oh yeah!" I shouted. "Have you talked to Bogey in the Pro Shop? That guy and I were just fine until you went and wrote that stupid article. Now, he thinks I killed a golfer on his course."

Jeff stopped for a moment, letting the thought sink in. "No way. How could he possibly believe that you…"

I shrugged. "It's scary, isn't it? When the words you write hold the power to change someone's mind, no matter how absurd those words may seem. Believe it or not, Jeffery Toobin, you have written something that is touching the minds and hearts of your fellow man. It's just a shame that what you're choosing to do is put out a bunch of tabloid-level gossip that, in the end, will render you a liar whom nobody will ever believe again."

Without giving him time to respond, I headed for my car. I hadn't found anything new that would prove my innocence, but I was sure as anything not going to stand there looking for clues with Jeff.

As I reached my car, my phone buzzed, alerting me I had a new email from Sheila Robinson.

I decided to do what I should have done the other day — I ignored it.

_____

11

Dear God,

It's me, Connie. I know you already knew that, but I have to ask you a question. And I know you already know what I'm going to say, but, dear Lord, and Sweet Baby Jesus, please just let me say it out loud to get it off my chest.

What the heck are you doing to me?

I mean really, God?!? What in the good name of all that is decent and holy are you doing to me right now?

Murder?

Really?

Am I to believe that this is part of your plan for me? That somehow the good people of Coffee Creek are supposed to look at me like I'm even the least bit capable of taking someone's life…which I'm not!

But again, you already know that.

I just can't figure you out, God. I want to have faith that this is going to be okay and that I'm supposed to learn something from this…but holy cow, this is a sucker punch in the gut.

I can't even breathe when I get thinking about what this could mean for my life here.

Answer me this, if you can. Am I gonna go to prison?

Because I feel like you and I are tight, Lord. I feel like we've been thick as thieves, pardon the expression. I know you're not a thief. But, you get the idea. You know that I'm your faithful servant, don't you?

Am I not on the right path? Is that what this is about? What am I supposed to do? 'Cause right now, I'm just a touch confused about what my purpose is here in this world.

Was I supposed to buy that building last year and take the financial risk and open up my own shop? Was I supposed to stop writing for the paper and all that other stuff?

Is this somehow your way of telling me to get on with my life and do something for myself?

Because if it is, God, you've got a funny way of communicating. But what if it's not that?

Oh my goodness, Lord, do you see what you are doing to me here? Do you?

I am trying so hard to figure this out. I am putting my neck on the line to clear my name. And I'm taking verbal bullets from The Gazette in the form of nasty articles dragging my name through the mud.

Verbal bullets, I tell ya!

And do you think there's going to be any way that I bounce back from this? Do you think that I can open up Connie's Cafe in Coffee Creek now?

No.

People are gonna look at me and think — well, first of all, half of them aren't going to look at me because they'll be afraid of me. But the ones that do dare encounter me in their travels are gonna walk away from me and say to themselves, 'It's amazing that that frail little thing had enough strength to go and kill a man.'

Is that what you want, Lord?

And I'm sorry, God, that I'm ranting like this, but I am just beside myself and I don't really know who I can talk to about this. I can't go to the police 'cause they're watching me. And I can't go to Sheila and Jeff 'cause they're writing about me. And I can't really go to Reba because…

Well, I can't think of a good reason I can't go to Reba.

You know what, Lord? I'm gonna go to Reba and see if she can help.

Thanks for the talk, and thanks for listening. I know it wasn't easy, because, Lord, oh, Lord what you're putting me through right now is crazy.

I want you to know, before I get off the line, here, that I love you God, and your son Jesus, and that Holy Spirit that's living inside of me. I'm having a little trouble locating it right at the moment, but I know it's in there.

I love all of you, and in all of you I put my trust and faith and life, and I am just praying to you now that you know what you're doing with all of this.

Okay, that's enough from me right now.

Thank you, dear God and Jesus,
In your holy name, I pray,
AMEN

12

A fter my drive-by prayer, and getting all of that out of my system, I drove over to Reba's apartment. Thursday was one of her days off during the week, so I figured she'd be there.

I hadn't been over to Reba's many times, but I had been there enough over the years to find it without having to use my GPS.

We'd gotten together a few times to have a girls' night, where we'd had shrimp cocktail, cheese and crackers, and some fruity drinks. Watching cheesy romcoms and talking about the men of our dreams were always on the menu, too.

She, like my mother and I, lived on the outskirts of Coffee Creek. And like the back nine of the golf course, her apartment was located on Route 37. It was about ten

minutes away from where I'd parked my car to go investigating.

I pulled into a stone driveway, kicking up dust as I
pulled up next to the house in one of the quasi-designated
parking spots.

Reba's apartment was the upstairs of a blue house.
There was a set of two-tiered steps leading up to a massive
deck. At the end of the deck was a gas grill and a bench,
next to the door.

I rang the doorbell and waited, feeling the cool breeze
as it rushed over my skin. Despite all of the things going
wrong in my life, I felt surprisingly better. Talking with
God often did that for me, even if I was verbally sparring
with him. Sometimes those tough conversations just had to
happen.

Speaking of tough conversations…

Reba came to the door after a few moments. Her hair
was still wet and draped on the back of a pink T-shirt.

"Well, good morning," she said, stepping out onto the
deck. "Nice of you to call."

"Sorry about that. I wasn't planning on coming over, it
just sort of happened. Call it *Divine intervention*."

She sat down on the bench next to the door. "Well,
you might as well have a seat and look out into the great
field of nothing with me."

I sat down and looked out over the railing of the deck.
Across the road was a field of grass, grown tall and wispy,
and blowing from left to right. There were little patches of

white and yellow flowers throughout. I, personally, thought that there could be worse views.

"So, what do you need?" Reba asked. She'd crossed her legs, and folded her hands on her lap. I could see her left foot twitching up and down, rhythmically.

"I need your help," I said. "But first, I have to apologize for not telling you what was bothering me the other day."

"Apology accepted," Reba fired off sharply.

"No," I said, turning to face her on the bench. I would have normally put my hands over hers, but I thought that might be a step too far, given Reba's mood. "I'm really sorry. I should have told you what was wrong and let you help, instead of shutting you out."

"Well, I agree." She stared glassy-eyed out toward the field.

"It's been a few days. I'm sure by now you've heard or read some things."

"Oh, yeah, I have," she nodded. "It's been all over the place. The local news, the papers, out of every mouth of every person that orders their morning coffee."

"That's what I figured. You know I didn't do anything wrong, right?"

She turned her face in my direction, staring at me with her alluring blue eyes. "Do you think I'd be sitting out here, alone, in a dripping wet T-shirt and slippers if I thought you'd killed anyone?"

"That's a good point," I chuckled.

"So, what are you doing here? Do you think I'm going to help you catch the bad guy or something?"

"Actually…" I bit my bottom lip. "I was hoping you might be willing to lend a hand."

"Okay." She responded much more quicker than I expected.

"Okay? Just like that?"

"Yeah," she nodded. "I've been waiting for you to ask me. You might not know this about me, but I'm a bit of a mystery hound."

"You are?" I was shocked. After all these years knowing Reba, the bubbly, goofy, sometimes less-than-motivated person I'd grown to love, I would not have taken her for one who enjoyed solving mysteries.

"Don't look so shocked," she said, pointing a finger at the side of her head. "There's a lot more in there than Caramel Macchiato and Chai Tea recipes, ya know."

"Great," I smiled. "So, what have you come up with so far?"

REBA SET two hot cups of steaming black coffee down on her kitchen table, next to a plate of homemade chocolate chip cookies. "Dillon loves these cookies, and they're supposed to be for him … but as soon as he gets home and cleans up those dishes, I'll make him some more. Go ahead, dig in. I'll be right back."

She disappeared through the doorway that led to the living room, which led to the rest of the apartment.

I took a moment to survey the kitchen. It made me smile on the inside. As it turns out, Reba at home was just like Reba at work. There were dishes strewn about on the counter and piled high in the sink. Droplets of coffee that had been spilled went untouched, and the bowls and measuring spoons that Reba had used to make the cookies were everywhere. The baking sheet was still on top of the stove, full of little tiny crumbs.

Dillon must be the best man in the world, I mused.

"How're the cookies?" Reba asked, coming back into the room with a spiral-bound notebook. It was smaller than most notebooks I'd seen and the paper looked pretty rough.

"I was waiting for you," I lied. I didn't want to tell her that I was admiring her for having a boyfriend that would come home from work and clean up her mess. "What kind of paper is that?" I asked, both to change the subject, but also because I'd never seen anything like it before in my life.

"Oh, this?" She held the notebook up and began leafing through the pages so I could get a good look at how no two pages were ever the same. "You're not going to believe this," she smiled, getting the craziest look in her eyes. "This paper is sourced from India, and it's made out of elephant poop."

I crinkled my nose at that information. *"Elephant poop?"*

"Yup. Apparently, it's quite a process. But it doesn't stink at all." She held the notebook out toward my face. "Here, smell."

"No thanks." I backed away as far as I could in the chair I was in. "I'll take your word for it."

"Ok," she said, pulling the notebook back toward herself, looking mighty disappointed in me. "Suit yourself."

"Can I ask a question?"

"You just did," she winked. "But if you'd like one more, I'd totally grant you that wish."

"Gee, thanks," I chuckled and took a sip of my coffee. Considering Reba worked in a coffee shop with me, I'd have guessed that she would have made a better cup of Joe. But, I also understood that she and Dillon were saving up for a someday wedding and house, which meant that she probably had to skimp somewhere. After my first sip of coffee, I could pretty much guarantee that she was saving money by buying cheap coffee beans. "Why would you buy paper made from animal dung? Like, is that a *thing*?"

"First, that's two questions. Second, it is a *thing*, as you so eloquently put it. Third, I buy it because if they make paper out of poop then they don't have to cut down trees."

I nodded reflectively. "That makes sense. I think I'll stick with the old-fashioned paper-making process, though."

"We'll see about that," she smirked. "You just might

find a little bit of elephant poop paper in your stocking for Christmas this year!"

We shared a laugh. Hers was a tad on the maniacal side like she was a villain who was just bound and determined to get her revenge on me somewhere down the line. Mine was as dismissive as I could make it without being rude, while still driving home the point that I didn't want to bury a ballpoint pen in some elephant's leavings.

Reba sat down and opened her notebook. She took a swig of her coffee and breathed in a very deep, satisfied breath. "There is absolutely nothing like homemade coffee."

"I know what you mean," I said, choking down a second sip.

"So, let's get down to business here. I've started making some notes of my own. First off, 'twas a golfer who died, and a very good golfer at that. A very good golfer, a few days before a major tournament. Local as it may be, the Coffee Creek Golf Tournament had a payout of twenty-thousand dollars for the winner. I'm going to go out on a limb here and say that it's quite possible it may have been a golfer who killed him."

"That's a pretty sturdy limb," I agreed.

"Have you ever met this guy's wife?"

"No," I said. It occurred to me that in the past three days, I had met so many people in Coffee Creek that I didn't even know existed. "I'm surprised at how few people I actually know in town."

"Well, you are kind of a hermit. No offense."

"What do you mean I'm a hermit? I go out and do things!"

"Like what? Work, church, groceries?"

"Yeah," I blushed. "Those are things."

"You're right," Reba chided. "Those are things. They just aren't the most social of things. They aren't exactly things that are going to get you meeting people."

"I guess you're right," I said, turning my head to stare out the window that was next to the kitchen table. All I could see was miles of road and field, and if I looked very hard I could make out Gustafson's Farm in the distance.

"I know I'm right. You know what would get you meeting more people?"

"What?"

"Opening up that little coffee shop you always talk about. That would get you to meet a ton of people. There are a few properties on Main Street that are for sale. They're right in the middle of everything, plus everyone loves their coffee. Am I right? Or am I right?"

"You're right," I nodded. "Before I can open up a coffee shop I've got to get my name cleared first, though. As it is, my big old face was on the front page of the paper yesterday with the word 'murderer' attached to it. I think, at this point, meeting people and setting up a cafe will have to come later."

"So, let's find out who Mr. David Gardner was

married to and we can talk to her. Maybe she knows something about the person that killed her husband."

"Sounds like a great plan. How do we find out who she is? The man who owns the golf course won't even look at me, let alone give me any information. Sheila and Jeff at the paper are writing awful stories about me as we speak, so they probably won't be a tremendous help. And the rest of the people in town are reading the articles that Jeff and Sheila are writing, so they'd probably run the other way if they saw me coming."

"Those are all good points, but I'm afraid you aren't thinking creatively enough."

"Oh really," I scoffed. "Well, how would you go about finding out who David Gardner's wife is?"

Reba's eyes opened as wide as I'd ever seen them before. They were like a couple of saucers with vibrant blue rings in the center. "Is your little black dress clean?"

13

"I can't believe I let you talk me into this," I said, elbowing Reba as we walked up the sidewalk to the *First Presbyterian Church of Coffee Creek*.

This was not my normal church, as I'd been raised Methodist. My mother and I continued going to that church, located a block away after my father passed.

"I don't know what the problem is," Reba replied, giving me a gentle nudge in the back. "One step at a time, one breath at a time. That's all there is to it."

My shoe touched the first step of five, as we approached the front door. The church was a beautiful white building with a tall steeple and bells at the top of the entryway.

"I can't do this," I whispered out the side of my mouth. "This feels disingenuous."

"It is," Reba continued to shove. "But people are starting to stare, so you'd better get on with it already."

I took a deep breath and walked up the rest of the steps and into the front door of the church, shaking a man's hand on the way in. I'd never seen him before in my life, but he was holding the door open for everyone and shaking their hands. Not wanting to stand out, I thought it would be good form to offer my hand as well.

As we moved through the entryway, we walked through another door and into the sanctuary, which opened up considerably. There were curved pews all facing a beautifully decorated altar and pulpit. There was a large organ directly behind the altar, and an old woman who I recognized from a story I once wrote about the apple pies of Coffee Creek. She'd told me that she'd never won a pie-baking contest, but everyone loved what she had to bake, and she couldn't argue with that. I think her name was Millie.

Once inside, I walked quickly behind the back row of pews until we got as far away from the entryway as possible. I then took a seat on the very edge. Reba climbed over me and sat down.

"Where do you think she is?" Reba asked, craning her neck and chomping on a piece of gum I'd asked her to throw away ten minutes earlier.

"Can you please stop and try to be a little more discreet?"

"Oh, please, you're just paranoid," Reba said, winking

at me. "Nobody's going to pay any attention to us back here."

If only that had been the case.

Within five minutes of Reba uttering those fateful words, Officer Theodore Billings walked into the church, dressed in his Sunday best. He was with a man I'd never seen before. The man was also dressed well, though he had more of a belly than Billings. He also had a very bushy, gray mustache and his hair was a rather floppy mop that was in the latent stages of salt and pepper.

Before they took their seats, Officer Billings made a beeline for me.

"I didn't expect to see you here," he said, as he approached.

I could feel my face turn bright red. "I didn't expect to be here."

"Listen," he said, "I know things didn't go great the other day at the station. I wanted to tell you that even though you're technically a suspect, none of us believe you are capable of anything like that."

I didn't know whether to feel relieved at his vote of confidence, or beyond angry that they had dragged me into this whole thing to begin with.

"That's nice," I said, curtly.

"I wanted to introduce you to someone," he said, standing and shooting an upward-facing palm at the man he'd walked in with. "This is Detective William Tolbert. He works for the county. He's here to help us out with this one. 'Cause let's face it, nothing like that ever happens around here, and we're a bit over our skis if you know what I mean." He winked.

Gag me, I thought. *A bit over our skis. No kidding.*

"Nice to meet you," I said, giving him my fingertips, and remaining seated. "I hope you do your job better than our local guys."

"I will do my best," he bowed his head. "But, with all due respect, I don't think this is the best setting to be having this discussion. If you don't mind, I'm going to excuse myself and find my seat."

He turned on his heel and walked toward the front of the church, sitting down in the center of the third row. Office Billings awkwardly nodded and followed Detective Tolbert to his seat.

"Can you believe that?" Reba asked. "*Nobody thinks you did it.*" She mocked. "Lotta nerve, that guy."

"Not here," I said, putting my hand on Reba's leg. "Please. It's bad enough that I let you drag me into this. Let's just get through it and get out of here as soon as possible."

"Roger, boss."

A door to our left opened, and a woman dressed all in black walked through it. She appeared to be in her early fifties. She was slender, with long flowing blond hair. Her makeup was impeccably done, and she was stone-faced, with not a tear in sight. Just in case, however, she was holding a tiny stack of pocket tissues in her left hand, which was adorned with a black silk glove. She was being escorted by the man I'd spoken to at the golf course before driving out to meet up with David Gardner.

What was his name again?

Chester Frank!

The owner of *Chester's High-End Jewelry*. Why would he be helping David Gardner's wife? He'd had nothing good to say about the deceased.

"Did you bring that poop paper?" I asked Reba.

"Sure did," she smiled, pulling it out of her purse and opening it up. "What am I writing down?"

"Write down the name, *Chester Frank*."

"Got it. What are you thinking?"

"I don't know just yet. But there's something about him that all of the sudden doesn't seem right."

"Are you gonna tell me now?" Reba asked as we piled into my car and pulled away from the church.

"Yes," I sighed. "Now that we are out of the funeral, and away from everyone, I can have a private conversation with you. Honestly, have you ever been to church? Do you know how people behave in places of worship — particularly when people are paying their respects to a person who's passed away?"

"I don't know what you're so mad about," Reba chortled. "That guy must have been really despised. Didn't you notice how few people were there to pay their respects?"

"I did."

It was true.

And sad.

Aside from his wife, Chester Frank, Officer Billings, Detective Tolbert, the pastor, Reba, and myself, there were maybe three or four other people present. I hadn't recognized any of them. Perhaps, they were family that had come from out of town.

"So, Chester Frank," Reba said, changing directions in the conversation. "What's the deal?"

"I don't know if there is a deal. But the other day when I spoke to him, he was spewing some serious venom about David Gardner, and what a horrible human being he was. Now, for him to show up at the man's funeral…on his wife's arm, no less. Something seems off about him. That's all."

"Yeah," Reba nodded, still smacking on her gum in the passenger seat. "That does sound weird. You should probably go and talk to him tomorrow."

"That's what I was thinking."

"Do you want me to go with you? I could try to get the morning off, or you could wait for the afternoon and we could go together. Totally up to you."

As much as I was enjoying all of this time with Reba, and she had certainly given my investigation the jump start that it needed, I wasn't quite sure that having her tag along was necessarily the best idea in the world.

"I think I can do it on my own," I said. Her face went dark in an instant and she turned away from me and began looking out the window.

Great, I thought. *Now Reba's mad at me…again. What else could go wrong this week?*

14

I was up and at 'em early the next morning, rifling through some scripture, trying to find some inspiration.

Going to *Chester's High End Jewelry* and chatting up the owner about how he may, or may not, have killed the only golfer standing in his way of twenty-thousand dollars, not to mention, the blond bombshell of his dreams, was not something I was looking forward to.

But it had to be done. I couldn't just sit around and wait for Officer Billings and Detective Tolbert to clear my name.

Even if I was found innocent, how many days of articles would *The Gazette* publish about me. If they wrote enough articles about how I was the possible killer of David Gardner, then it didn't matter what the truth was.

There would still be a big part of the Coffee Creek population that believed I was a murderer.

I had to stop the bleeding.

As I was pouring coffee into a travel mug, my phone buzzed in my back pocket.

"Hello," I answered. My voice was surprisingly chipper and bright.

"Hi, Connie? This is Officer Billings."

The chipper and bright was suddenly on the urge of turning dower and dark.

"Yes…"

"Have you seen the article in *The Gazette* today?"

"No, I haven't."

"Well, allow me to fill you in." His voice was short and irritable. "On the front page, there's a picture of you on the golf course — looking very shocked, and, dare I say, guilty. Below the picture is a caption that reads, 'Connie Cafe goes back to the scene of the crime two days after the murder of David Gardner.'"

I was speechless.

"Would you like me to go on?" Billings continued without waiting for my response. "The article goes into great detail about how you and Jeff Toobin had a chance encounter at the scene of the grisly murder, and how you were searching for clues that the police had missed because, and I quote, 'the police in this town are simply incompetent, and if it's up to those bumbling buffoons I will rot in a prison cell for the rest of my life', end quote."

"That's not at all what I said!" I tried to defend myself against even more false accusations. But who was I kidding? Just like with David Gardner's murder, nobody was around to hear me say, or not say, those words. It was my word against *The Gazette's*, and at this point, it seemed like most people were siding with them.

"Enlighten me," Officer Billings challenged. "Go ahead and tell me exactly what you said."

"I didn't say anything to him," I answered. "Not about the police, anyway."

There was silence on the other end of the line. I took the opportunity to pop the top on the travel mug and grab my keys.

"Connie," Billings finally said, "I need you to back out of this one, as hard as it may seem. It really doesn't look good for you to be mucking around, conducting your own investigation. Not to mention that if we are conducting an investigation, then your investigation is illegal and could get you into a lot of trouble."

"So, I'm just supposed to sit back and wait while this guy keeps writing horrible things about me? The whole town thinks I killed a guy. And, by the way, not that it was pleasant, but David Gardner's murder was most certainly not grisly. That is complete hyperbole."

"I understand how upsetting this must be." His voice was suddenly soft and compassionate. "But I am urging you to take a few steps back and trust the system. We've got a good investigator here in Tolbert. He's already made a lot of headway. Just give him some time."

"Thank you for your call," I said. I had heard and fully understood his message loud and clear. But I had things to do…and waiting around wasn't one of them.

"So you're going to cool it a little?" He asked.

"If that's what you think is best."

"It is."

"Have a great day," I said.

"You too, Connie."

I hung up and put the phone back in my pocket. Coffee and keys in hand, I headed out the door to go give Chester Frank a visit.

CHESTER'S SHOP was located on Main Street. I rarely, if ever came down here, though I really wanted to be here every day.

My father and I had had many talks about the proud men and women who owned businesses on this street. He'd told me on more than one occasion that these people and places were the life blood of Coffee Creek.

I had so badly wanted a place down here. There were a few buildings vacant, but there was something within, holding me back from acting on my dream. Now, with *The Gazette* plastering my face across the front page every day, my imaginary dragon seemed farther away than ever. In fact, it seemed like a big gust of wind had come in unexpectedly and blown the whole cloud apart, wisp after wisp blown off into different directions, never to be reformed.

Main Street had everything. It had a bookstore, a bakery, a pub, a pizza shop, a florist, a seafood restaurant, an antique shop, a bank, a toy store, a small movie theater, a deli, a comedy club, and a theater for stage productions, a small gazebo overlooking the creek…but no coffee shop.

The big box shop I worked at had come in a few years ago and filled a void. But I knew that if I could just get started, I'd be able to make a killing selling coffee on Main Street because my coffee would be better and my place would have real heart.

But that was neither here, nor there.

Chester's High-End Jewelry was located at the far end of the street, between the *Coffee Creek Pub & Grub* and the *Coffee Creek Laugh Shack*. It was a narrow building, with a reddish-brown brick face and a massive display window. Looking at it from the sidewalk, the brown metal framed door was on the right-hand side. The glass on the window had an ethereal kind of scroll:

Chester's
High End
Jewelry
We've got you covered!

Below the shop's slogan was a list of hours. Chester

opened the shop Tuesday through Saturday from 8 AM to 9 PM.

By the time I'd arrived, the place had been open for about an hour.

I walked in and was taken aback by how much jewelry he was able to fit into such a small place and not have it feel cluttered. The display case wrapped around the entire store, with a separate case in the middle of the square room. A few shelves were hung on the wall with various cleaning and polishing products.

Chester was standing next to the cash register, examining a ring that was missing a stone.

"Welcome to Chester's," he said, not looking up. "Is there anything I can help you with?"

"Well," I said, approaching him. "I'm not really here about jewelry."

He placed the ring down on the glass top of the display case. I was amazed at how gently he handled the dainty piece.

Looking up at me for the first time, he snapped his fingers, and pointed, his hand bouncing like his wrist had a hinge in it. "I remember you…hold on, don't tell me."

He snapped a few more times, closed his eyes, and bobbed his head up and down. "You're that chick from the newspaper, right?"

Chick, huh? Interesting approach from a guy who makes his living selling jewelry for *chicks*.

I thought it best not to make too big a deal out of it. I

wanted answers, and if my time at the paper had taught me anything, it's that you catch more flies with honey.

"That's me," I replied, holding out my hand. He shook it. "Connie Cafe."

"Right," he said, taking his hand back and slapping his forehead. "I'd forget my head if it wasn't attached."

Oh, brother, I thought. *Chicks and Cliches, this guy had it all going his way.*

"What can I do ya for?"

Wow.

"I was actually hoping to talk to you about David Gardner," I said, getting right to the point.

"Oh," he said, standing up, his face and demeanor sobered in a hurry. "Good man, David. Very sorry to hear about what happened. Tragic, really. You know," he said, looking me in the eyes, a sudden hammed-up intensity to his stare. "You really do have to appreciate every day you're given by the good Lord because you just never know when it's going to be your last. Know what I mean?"

I nodded. "I know exactly what you mean."

"So, what do you want to know about David?"

"Well, I noticed that you were at the funeral the other day."

His eyes changed instantly as shock came across his face momentarily before fading to a feigned calm and cool.

"David was a friend," he said. "Why wouldn't I be there?"

"Of course, I understand. I guess I was just wondering who that woman on your arm was."

He shifted uncomfortably putting his weight on his right foot. "That was David's Wife, Brenda," he replied. "She asked me to accompany her. She thought it would be too painful to go by herself."

"I see," I said, moving along the display case, and checking out his ring selection. "And have you known Brenda long?"

"Since we were kids," he nodded. "We went to school together."

"And you were friends with David and Brenda? Or just Brenda?"

I knew I was getting a bit bold with my questions, but I wanted to really dig. My presumed innocence was on the line.

"What are you getting at? Are you writing an article or something for that paper of yours?"

"No," I shook my head. I held my empty hands up. "I don't even have my trusty notebook and pen."

"Then why are you so interested in my personal relations?"

"Well," I said, turning and walking back toward the register. "I distinctly remember you saying that you thought David Gardner was…how did you put it? Oh yeah," I said, snapping my fingers. "A real S.O.B. Isn't that what you said?"

"I'm failing to understand why that has anything to do with this little exchange we're having."

Little beads of sweat were starting to form on his brown, and I could sense a slight quiver in his voice.

"Wouldn't it seem odd to you if you met a person who once said horrible things about this other person? And then as soon as this other person passes away, under, what could arguably be deemed suspicious circumstances, the person who said all of the horrible things shows up at the funeral of the deceased with the deceased's wife on his arm?"

I moved for the door. "Because, that seems mighty odd to me, Mr. Frank."

"I think you've been watching too much TV. Either that or you've been hanging out with that hack editor, Sheila Robinson, for far too long. Either way, you're coming off as crazy and desperate." He stepped out from around the register and put his hands on his hips. "I know what they've been writing about you. And I'm going to let you know that if you, in any way, try to drag my name into this, you're going to look more foolish and guilty than you already do."

"Is that a threat?"

"No," he smiled. "It's a guarantee."

With that, I walked out of his shop and into the warm May breeze. That hadn't gone exactly as I'd hoped, but now, I at least knew David Gardner's wife had a name.

And it was time to go pay Brenda a visit.

15

My legs were a little shaky as I walked up the brick sidewalk that connected the Gardner's quaint raised ranch-style house to a small, but pristinely manicured front lawn and short, paved driveway.

Dear God,

Please give me the strength, oh Lord, to be a tool for good and to find the words to communicate clearly with this grieving woman.

Thy will be done.

AMEN

Before I'd even knocked, Brenda was standing in the doorway. She was staring at me through the screen, her blond hair flanking her cheeks and resting on her shoulders. She was wearing what I would consider a rather swanky dress, vibrant yellow, with a very shiny white pearl necklace draped across her chest.

I'd made a mental note that she had not been wearing any visible jewelry at the funeral the day before. Maybe that was just her style when mourning and grieving. Then again, maybe something else was going on.

"May I help you?" She asked as I approached the steps. I did not step up onto them, as I thought that might be a step too far.

"Yes," I said. "I'm Connie Cafe, and I live out on Route 14 on the other side of Coffee Creek. I'm the woman who found your husband the other day. I saw you at the funeral, and I just wanted to stop by and tell you personally how truly sorry I am for your loss."

"Well, that's nice of you," she threw a quick smile in my direction and then put it away just as fast as she'd taken it out. "If you don't mind, I'm just leaving now."

I didn't know why I was so surprised that she was going somewhere. It wasn't like her life was over because her husband had just died. At the same time, it did seem a tad odd.

"Okay, well, have fun!" I called out as I turned and headed for my car.

Have fun?!?!

Was that really the best thing I could think of? Apparently, it was.

I reached my car and pulled out of the driveway, slightly embarrassed. But even more than embarrassed, I was curious. Where was this newly widowed woman going, the day after her husband's funeral, dressed like that?

Every essence of my being was telling me to leave it alone, to just go home. *Don't follow her*, my mind was telling my heart. But, as is often the case, my heart didn't listen. Rather, it gave my mind a Judo chop right in the face.

Dear Lord,

I'm calling on you right now for what I would like to call preemptive forgiveness.

You've known me all my life, and I'm sure you already know what I'm about to do. Maybe, you're even up there watching me at this moment, wishing that I'd just stop following Brenda's car into town. I can almost hear you in my ear, telling me that I should just stop what I'm doing and go home already and trust in you because you've never let me down before.

But Lord, it's not you I don't trust. It's Officer Billings and Detective Tolbert; It's Jeff Toobin and Sheila Robins; It's Chester Frank and Brenda Gardner.

And Lord, my God, I know you've given each and every one of them free will, and right now, it seems to me that they are using their free will in a way that is making my life kind of miserable.

Have you ever been accused of murder?

I'm sorry. I suppose that's probably a dumb question, given the trials and tribulations that you put your son, Jesus, through. I'm sure many people have asked you the question about why you killed your own son.

I guess this is what Jesus meant when he said, "Before they have persecuted you, they persecuted me." Yeah, that all makes sense now.

But still, God, I've got to find out what's going on here in this whole murder thing that you've gone and gotten me all wrapped up in.

So, if what I'm doing is wrong, I'm going to preemptively ask you for forgiveness, for I know not what I do.

On the other hand, if this is what I am supposed to be doing, God, give me the strength to stay steadfast and determined, and hope that I catch whoever killed that man.

In your holy name, I pray.

AMEN

16

I had given Reba a call and asked her to meet me downtown for lunch at the *Coffee Creek Pub & Grub*.

"And why should I do that?" She'd asked in that sassy way she has.

"Because I'm paying," I told her.

That was all it took. She was at the restaurant in less than ten minutes. I'd been sitting on a bench out in front of the place, reading a book, holding it up to my face as close as possible in hopes that no one would see me.

"What are you doing?" Reba laughed as she walked up the sidewalk.

"Can you keep it down?" I hushed her. "I don't want anyone to know I'm here."

"Oh," she said, looking around, craning her neck in all

directions. "I think you're clear. The street's dead this morning. Besides, it's not even eleven-thirty yet."

"I know that," I said. "I'm just a little on edge right now, okay?"

"Sure, fine. Whatever." She pulled a hair tie out of her pocket and began putting her flowing, purple locks into a tight ponytail. "Honestly, this darn wind is screwin' up my hair, and I don't like it. So why are you having lunch at the *P&G* if you don't want to be seen by anyone? Wouldn't it just be easier to eat at home and avoid this scene altogether?"

"Yes," I mused, "I suppose it would. But I needed to talk to you and I thought the best way to get back into your good graces would be to buy you a nice lunch."

"Oh," she rolled her eyes, "I see. This is straight-up bribery."

"Not exactly," I smiled. "I'm also having a wicked hankering for their haddock sandwich and a beer."

"Well, what are we waiting for?" She said, moving toward the narrow, flower-lined sidewalk that led to the front door of the restaurant. "Let's go eat!"

THE *COFFEE CREEK PUB & Grub* was a beautiful small-town bar and grill. The lighting was dim, and the wood-work was dark and slick. It was a town favorite for quick, business lunches and long, family dinners alike. After dark, it became a singles hang out, where drinks were cheap and decisions were questionable. Needless to say, it was quite the hit, and business had never been better.

Our waitress was Penny Simpson. She and I had graduated high school together. Penny had been the class Valedictorian, but after leaving the small town of Coffee Creek, the real world had proven just how big and vicious it could be when provided with enough opportunities.

Penny came back in shame, a pregnant college dropout with no idea who the father was.

The years since had been tough on her, and she wore every day of those years across her face.

"Hey Connie," she waved, as Reba and I approached the waiting area. "Two?"

"Yes, thank you."

"Outside or in?"

I looked at Reba. "Can your hair handle it?" I smiled and winked, just to let her know I was kidding.

"Ha, ha, very funny," she grumbled. "Outside would be fine," she told Penny.

Penny grabbed two menus and said, "Follow me." We walked with her through the bar and indoor dining room. There were a few guys sitting at the bar, dressed in suits, drinking beer from frosted pint glasses, and watching sports on the flat-screen TVs. They were, no doubt, writing this off as a business expense.

The dining room was empty as it was still a little on the early side for lunch. All of the tables were set with silverware wrapped in black cloth napkins and empty water glasses.

As we walked through, toward the French doors that opened out onto the large deck, I admired the artwork that adorned the walls. It was mostly paintings of large boats on the sea. I was amazed at the faith the men who guided those ships must have had, to be all alone out in the middle of the ocean, where if anything happened, they were at the mercy of the sea.

They were nice reminders that no matter how out to sea it seemed like I was, no matter how alone I felt, I was in God's hands and I would be taken care of.

"Do you have a preference?" Penny's raspy voice snapped me back to reality. She was holding out her arm, moving it in a half circle, showing us that any seat we wanted could be ours.

"How about over there?" Reba pointed to a small table for two next to the railing. "I don't know about you, Connie, but I love to sit as close to the Creek as possible."

"Sounds like a plan," I nodded.

"Do you need some time to look? Or do you know what you want already?" Penny asked as we took our seats.

"I'm dying for that haddock sandwich you guys make. And I'll have a glass of Blue Moon."

"Good choice." Reba flipped through the menu quickly, before closing it. "I'll have the same as Connie."

We handed our menus to Penny and she went back inside.

"So what's really going on?" Reba asked as soon as the French doors closed and we were alone.

"I saw something this morning and I wanted to get your take on it."

"What's that?"

I leaned in close and brought my voice down to a near whisper. "I went to visit Chester Frank today. He claims that he's been friends with David Gardner's wife, Brenda since they were in school together."

"Okay."

"He tried to tell me that he was friends with both of them and that's why Brenda was on his arm at David's funeral."

"Okay."

"But he told me that David was a real S.O.B. the other day at the golf course. He also told me that if it wasn't for David, he'd have won the tournament for the last few years. Reba, that's twenty thousand dollars, per year, this man has lost out on because of David Gardner."

"So, what are you saying?" Reba asked. She raised her eyebrows. "Are you telling me that he killed the guy?"

"I don't know," I shrugged. "It's definitely possible. He was on the course at the same time as David. And the course was almost empty at the time. Anything could have happened back there in those trees, away from anyone's eyes."

"I don't know," Reba shook her head. "It sounds like a bit of stretch."

"I realize that, but that's not all."

"That's not all?" She mocked.

"No, there's more!"

"More, you say?" She leaned forward and put her chin in her hands. "Tell me all about it."

"I went over to Brenda Gardner's house."

"Really?" Reba sat up, and the jokey tone in her voice disappeared. "This is getting very serious."

"She was dressed in a bright yellow dress and a pearl necklace, done up to the nines, and hot to trot. And she wanted nothing to do with me."

"I can't say I blame her," Reba smirked. "I mean, the only reason I'm here is that you're paying."

"Oh, shut up," I laughed.

"So what did you do? Did you follow her like they do in the movies?"

I smiled across the table.

"You did not!" Reba leaned forward, folding her arms. "Connie, as much fun as this all sounds, you're going to get yourself into some serious trouble."

"Let me remind you, that you were the one who got out the poop paper yesterday and encouraged me to go out and do this."

"I did no such thing. I was talking about figuring things out on the pages of a notebook, not following widows through town, and visiting jewelers with an axe to grind. That's just nuts."

"Well, I'm in it now," I said, sitting back in my chair. "Do you want to know what I saw when I followed Brenda?"

Reba nodded. "I mean, since you went to all the trouble of tailing her through town, I think the least you could do is tell me what you saw."

"Thanks," I smiled. "She drove over to *Chester's High-End Jewelry*. When she arrived, I saw Chester open the door for her. They both looked down the street like they were trying to make sure that nobody was going to see what they were about to do. And then Chester closed the door and put a giant 'Closed' sign in the window."

"That does seem suspicious. It sounds like they may have just been having an affair," she said, nonchalantly.

"Don't you think that's a big deal? Doesn't that type of thing lead people to do awful things…like murder."

"Sure." Reba sat back and smiled. "If you believe everything you see on TV, then you might think that Chester and Brenda having fun behind David Gardner's back might be proof that they killed him. But, here, in the real world, sister, an affair is far from evidence of a crime."

Well, how do you like that? The person who encouraged me to get out there and prove my innocence was now the one telling me that my efforts were all mired in some small-town fantasy concocted by watching too many movies.

My phone buzzed. Another email from Sheila. I shook my head and turned my phone off.

Penny arrived with our sandwiches and beers, and I was suddenly not hungry.

17

I went home after lunch and laid in my bed, staring at the ceiling.

What if Reba had been right?

Maybe, Chester and Brenda having an affair was just that. Maybe, it was nothing more.

Why was I having such a hard time believing that?

The dots were all there, and as I ran through everything I'd discovered so far, they all seemed to connect.

Had Brenda loved Chester so much more than her husband that she'd asked him to kill David? Had Chester been so taken by Brenda that he'd actually done it? Had killing him on the golf course been a way of sending a message to the other golfers who might dare get in the way of him and his twenty thousand dollar prize?

It was all there. It all made perfect sense.

The problem: I had no real evidence like Reba said. This was the stuff of TV shows and mystery novels. Not real life.

I turned my phone on to see if anyone had tried to get a hold of me during the past three hours.

It buzzed about five times as email after email from Sheila flooded my inbox.

I rolled my eyes as they came in.

But then I started thinking that I might want to check them. She usually sent me a text if something were really important.

I checked my text messages — nothing.

That was odd.

When I opened my emails I was surprised at what I saw. Sheila, in typical Sheila fashion, had not intended to email me.

All of the emails in my inbox were group emails, to both me and Jeff Toobin. None of them had anything in the subject line. When I opened them, they were barely interpretable. It was almost like she was writing in code. And she was only writing to Jeff.

One of the emails read:

Jeff,

Is everything done?

~Sheila

Another one read:

Jeff,

Did you take care of it yet?

~Sheila

These struck me as incredibly odd. Sheila was a lot of things. Scatterbrained, disorganized, a fashion train wreck — all of these came to mind. What didn't come to mind, when I thought about Sheila, was cryptic. If anything, she was too honest and blunt to a fault.

What did these emails mean?

Reba was in my head. I could hear her telling me that I was just paranoid and that I should probably turn off my mind for a little bit and go experience the real world.

I had never been good at experiencing the real world. So, I did what any woman desperate to clear her name would do. I went to the police station in hopes of talking things over with Officer Billings and Detective Tolbert.

OFFICER BILLINGS and Detective Tolbert stood in the corner of Billings's office, staring at the emails on my phone.

"These do look suspicious," Tolbert said. He looked at

me and asked, "Does this woman usually communicate in such a hush, hush, short form sort of way?"

"Oh, no," I shook my head, perhaps, a little more dramatically than I needed to. "She's usually very verbose. She'll talk your ear off if you let her. Here," I said, reaching for my phone. I retrieved an earlier email from Shiela from my inbox and handed the phone back to Detective Tolbert. "This is what her typical email looks like."

"Wow," he said, his eyes wide with surprise. "That is quite a bit different than what we were just seeing, isn't it?" He turned to Officer Billings and joked, "It's honestly hard to believe that she can edit a newspaper. Take a look at all of the impertinent information she's included in this note."

They both shared a quick smile and then Detective Tolbert turned back to me.

"So, what are you thinking?"

"I don't know," I shrugged. "These two are writing horrible stories about me, smearing my name all over town, a man was killed a few days ago, and Chester Frank and Brenda Gardner look like they're having an affair. I don't know what to think anymore."

"Wait." Detective Tolbert held a hand up, stopping me from saying more. "How do you know about Chester and Brenda?"

I had said too much. Officer Billings had lost his smile

as his face transformed into a mixture of anger and disappointment.

"I'm sorry," I said. "But I've been accused of murder, here."

"No one has accused you of anything," Detective Tolbert said. He flashed Officer Billings a sharp look. "Being a suspect is far different than being accused."

"Well, from where I'm standing, it doesn't feel very different. Do you know what people are thinking about me every day after they open up their papers? They're reading those horrible articles about me." I was on the verge of tears as my eyes met Tolbert's. "*You* may not think I did it, but *they're* starting to. And it's all because of the two people in those emails."

There was a moment of tense silence as Tolbert thought things over. He sat down in a chair and stared at my phone.

After a few minutes, he said, "I think I have an idea."

18

The morning of the golf tournament was upon Coffee Creek, and the wheels were in motion to prove my innocence and find the true killer of David Gardner.

I went to the police station as the sun was just coming up. Tolbert and Billings were there already, waiting for me.

"You're sure you're up for this, Connie?" Billings asked. He was pacing back and forth, nervously. It was kind of sweet how worried he was about everything.

"I'll be fine," I smiled. "Whatever comes my way, it's worth clearing my name."

"She'll be fine," Tolbert assured Billings. "We'll be just around the corner if she needs us."

DEAR LORD,

    I certainly hope we're on the right track with this thing. Please keep all of us safe as everything plays out this morning.

    Thy will be done, Lord.

    Thy will be done.

WALKING up the steps to *The Gazette* felt strange. It had been five days since I'd last been there. I was sure that I would not be greeted with a warm welcome.

I opened the screen door and walked in like I still worked there. Sheila was her usual frantic self, and Jeff was drinking coffee and banging the keys on his computer in the back corner, no doubt writing his latest fictional account of Connie Cafe, Coffee Creek's most notorious killer.

"Well, look what the cat dragged in," Sheila smiled as she realized I was there. "What are you doing here?"

"Yeah," Jeff called out. "Shouldn't you be covering the tournament today? Or did they ban you from the course?" He chuckled to himself as he brought his styrofoam cup up to his lips.

"I'm here to talk to you about the articles you've been writing about me."

"What about them?" Sheila shrugged. "It's nothing personal, we're just doing our job, following the scoop. You know how that goes?"

"I thought I did," I said, stepping forward. "But you're not reporting honestly."

"What do you mean?" Sheila looked up, a smug look of feigned surprise plastered on her face. "Aren't you a suspect in the murder of David Gardner?"

"Technically, I am," I nodded. "But you know as well as I do that I'm only a suspect because I was the only one around when David Gardner was discovered."

"We're just reporting the truth as it unfolds," she smiled. "If that's all you're here to talk about, then I'm afraid we can't help you." She turned back to her paperwork.

"Actually, that's not all I'm here to talk about. I'm wondering if you could tell me about these emails between you and Jeff."

They both stopped what they were doing and stared at each other.

"What emails would you be referring to?" Sheila asked after a beat, her voice oddly distant.

"The ones with no subject lines that you sent to Jeff all week. Allow me to read." I took out my phone and pulled up my email. "Oh, like this one here, it says, 'Is everything done?'. That one was sent on Monday. Then there's this one that came on Wednesday. It says, 'Did you take care of it yet?'. There are a bunch of others too, and some really crazy ones that came in yesterday about 'nobody suspecting anything' and being 'in the clear'. But I'm guessing you already know about those."

Jeff stood up from behind his desk. He fired off a glance at Sheila, a fiery rage in his eyes. "What were you doing? You see me every day, you don't have to send me emails!"

"If you'd check your email every now and then we could have avoided this whole thing," she shouted.

"You're incompetent!" Jeff grunted as he passed Sheila and lunged at me.

I tried to move, but I wasn't quick enough. The next thing I knew, Jeff Toobin had thrown me over his shoulder and was heading out the side door of the office and down to his car.

I kicked and screamed as he fumbled with his keys in his pocket.

"This'll go better for you if you just hold still."

"I don't believe that for a second," I mustered. "You've lied every step of the way."

As we reached his car, he pressed a button and two loud beeps sounded as his trunk popped open.

He put me down.

"Get in the trunk," he ordered.

"I don't think so."

His shoulders were moving up and down rapidly as he tried to regain his breath.

"Come on," he said between heaves. "Get in, or it's going to get ugly."

"How so?" I asked, stalling for time. I just had to stall

long enough for Billings and Tolbert to arrive. Clearly, they'd heard enough to know I was in trouble.

"Like this," he said, pulling a black pistol from behind his back. He pointed it at me and motioned for me to get into the trunk again.

This time, I listened. I was sure to crawl in slowly, in hopes that my knights in shining armor would arrive.

"Hurry up," Jeff snarled, looking around like the paranoid snake that he was. "Get in before I shoot you!"

As I brought my left leg over the edge of the trunk, he shoved the rest of it in and slammed the trunk door down.

I was alone in the darkness, and I could make out the sound of his feet grinding against the gravel outside before his car door opened and shut. The engine came to life and I was thrust forward, and then back as he pulled out of his spot and turned out onto the road.

19

*D*ear Sweet Baby Jesus,

If this is the last thing I do on this earth, I'd just like to send up my gratitude to you, Lord, for a blessed life.

I'd also ask that you wrap your loving arms around my mother and find a way to help her through the tragedy of her daughter's murder at the hands of that deranged man behind the wheel.

I'm sorry, God. I know I shouldn't talk like that about a fellow child of yours. But you do have to kinda admit, that one's gone a bit wayward, wouldn't you say?

Is that considered the judgement of another?

If it is, oh, Lord, I hope you won't hold it against me too much when we meet at the gates of Heaven. I'm in a significant amount of distress at the moment. And the men who were supposed to be around to help me, seem to have turned up missing in my hour of need.

Then, again, maybe that was your plan all along. I don't know, and I will never claim to know what you have in store for me. But I do trust you. And if this is my time then I will happily accept it, and join you in eternal life.

If it's not my time, though, it would be nice if we could wrap this up fairly quickly because I don't know how much more of this adventure I can take, dear Lord.

And if my body bounces off another side of this trunk, so help me goodness, I don't know what I'm going to do. Honestly, this man is driving like a maniac. It's almost like he's being chased by someone...

Hey there, wait a minute! Did the boys in blue show up after all?

I know, I know. Let's not get too far ahead of ourselves now. I just need to take each moment as it's given to me. I'm just going to close my eyes and hope that my body can handle the thrashing it's taking at the moment.

And I know, dear God, that it's nothing like the savage torment and mockery that was bestowed upon your only son. I know that I could never be strong enough to handle such a thing, sweet Jesus.

You are my rock and my redeemer, and into your hands, I lay my life.

AMEN

20

The tires of Jeff's car stopped and slid hard, jolting me yet again.

I heard him open his door, but not close it. Then I heard more tires squealing and a great deal of yelling.

"Freeze!" I heard that from my less than cozy confines of Jeff Toobin's dark trunk. "Drop your weapon!"

After that, I heard a loud bang and instantly felt sick to my stomach.

Was that just a warning shot? If not, whose gun was it? And who had been shot, if anyone?

I waited silently, only the sound of my breath and my rapidly beating heart were audible.

I could hear someone groaning and whaling in pain.

At first, I wasn't sure who it was, but then I heard Officer Billing's voice shout, "Cuff him and get him outta here."

A few long moments later, the trunk popped open, and sunlight from the sky above flooded the once-black space.

I squinted my eyes and covered my face with my arm while contorting the rest of my body into the fetal position for protection—just in case.

"You can come out," the cheery voice of Officer Billings suggested. "No one's going to hurt you now."

It was just like that first day when he'd comforted me on the golf course. I felt so safe as he helped me from the trunk.

"Is he…?" I asked as I looked at Jeff Toobin's body, still and face down on the parking lot of the *Coffee Creek Gas and Guzzle.* His hands were cuffed and there was a small pool of blood around his foot.

"He's going to be fine," Officer Billings smiled. "He shot himself when he dropped his weapon."

"What?"

"I guess one could say that he shot himself in the foot."

We smiled and locked eyes.

"How can I ever thank you?" I asked.

"Well, for one," he said, "you can promise me that you're never going to get yourself into anything like this ever again."

"I promise," I smiled.

Detective Tolbert joined us after a few minutes. "Connie, we're going to need some statements from you so that we can get the paperwork right and put this derelict away for a while."

While I was talking to Detective Tolbert, Officer Billings had gone over to the trunk and was snooping around.

"Look what I found," he said, holding up a long metal stick with a small wire basket on the end of it. "I'm guessing the bruises on David's body will probably match the width of this."

"What is that?" I asked.

"It's a ball retriever," Detective Tolbert answered. "Most golfers aren't very good. And sometimes we lose our balls in the water. That stick is a tool that one might use to reach into slightly deeper depths to get their golf balls back. Golf balls aren't cheap — so, you do what you can. Let me see that for a second."

Officer Billings handed the ball retriever over and Detective Tolbert studied it closely. "Oh, yeah." He pointed to a point in the middle of it. "Do you see all those dents? They didn't get there by reaching this into the water to get golf balls, that much I can tell you."

He brought his eyes down toward the black rubber handle. "Well, would you look at that?"

"What is it?" Officer Billings stepped to his side and brought his eyes down to where Tolbert was pointing. "D.G. etched into the metal."

"Beaten to death with his own ball retriever," Tolbert

mused morosely. "What a shame."

"Okay," I interrupted. "I have some questions."

I turned and walked over to Jeff, who was still face down on the concrete. I sat next to him, not worried one bit about my white pants.

"Why did you do it?"

"I don't know," he breathed. "Sheila somehow convinced me that it would be a good idea. She told me that I could be the full-time writer at *The Gazette* and that if we could get a juicy enough story we'd make a ton of money. She was certain that we could get away with it too, what with his wife having an affair with Chester Frank and all of the other golfers hating him."

"You killed a man so you and Sheila would have an important story? That's the most disturbing thing I've ever heard."

"I didn't kill him," he retorted. "I hit him in the head a few times and he fell into the water. The water killed him."

I shook my head at the lengths that some people were willing to go to in order to avoid their own culpability.

"Did you guys get Sheila?" I called out to Officer Billings and Detective Tolbert.

They pointed to the blue squad car, the lights ablaze on the top of it. Sheila was sitting in the back seat, her makeup smudged on the window.

"What do you think took us so long to get to you?" Billings chuckled.

Real charmer, that one.

21

"Shut the front door!" Reba gasped when I told her what had happened.

I'd invited her over for dinner at our house. My mother, as usual, was a cooking fool. She'd made us broiled salmon with dill, over a bed of asparagus, and a side of polenta.

As usual, she'd picked a stunning wine to pair. Gewurtztraminer from Austria added some beautiful notes that highlighted the butter, and dill without overpowering the salmon.

"They didn't think anyone would miss him?" Reba sat back in her chair and finished her second glass of wine. "What a couple of wahoos. By the way, Mrs. Cafe, I'm not going to be able to drive home tonight because this wine is just too darn delicious."

"Oh, don't worry about that, dear. We have a spare bedroom and plenty of clothes in the closet if you'd like to stay the night." She winked at Reba and said, "Besides, there's more where that came from!"

Reba looked at my mother and said, "I like your style, Mrs. Cafe."

"Oh, please," my mother added. "Call me Roberta."

"Will do, Roberta," Reba laughed. She looked at me and asked, "Why can't you be as cool as your mother?"

"What's that supposed to mean? I just solved a murder for crying out loud. How much cooler can you get than that?"

"It certainly runs in the family," my mother noted.

I set my fork down and stared across the table at my mother. "What do you mean?"

"Oh, nothing. Just a story for a different time."

"Uh-uh." I shook my head. "Not a different time. This time."

"I'll tell you what. You, ladies, clean up the kitchen and meet me in the living room with another bottle of vino and I'll tell you the most amazing story about Connie's father and how he stopped a holiday heist."

Reba and I stared at my mother, our mouths agape.

"What?" I stammered. "I never heard anything about dad stopping any crimes."

"Oh, sure." My mother sat back and stared off blankly into space, reminiscing aloud. "He was one of the police department's favorite people. He had a real finger on the pulse of everything that was going on in town. I'll tell you what though, he was one lucky bugger. He almost got killed more than once. Why do you think we always made those cookies for the police? They saved your father's hide more than I care to remember."

Reba stood up quickly and started clearing the table before I'd even finished my last bite of salmon. She was like a child who'd been promised a piece of candy after dinner if she did the dishes well.

"Come on, slowpoke," she snapped at me. "What are you waiting for?"

"Alright," I said, standing up and joining in.

My mother grabbed my arm as I walked by. "I love you, pumpkin," she said. Her eyes had tears in them.

"I love you, too," I said, bending over and kissing the top of her head.

"What are you waiting for?" She asked.

"What do you mean?"

"I mean your dreams, Connie. I know you've got some money squirreled away, and you have no job at the paper to go back to, not to mention you've been given a second chance at life."

I looked away, but she tugged on my arm and pulled my attention back.

"I think it's time that you made your imaginary dragon a reality, don't you? Bet on yourself for once, kiddo! You're always doing things for other people."

"I'll think about it," I said.

"No, no, no," my mother's red hair shook back and forth. "You've *been* thinking about it. Now it's time to go out there and *do it*. You can hire Reba to help in the front. She's got experience. I can help you with the books if need be."

"Mom," I started to argue. Then my eyes met hers and I saw how much she believed in me.

"Make it happen, Connie." She pulled me close and whispered in my ear. "Make it happen."

A moment went by before I finally pulled away. We were both crying and nodding our heads fervently.

"I will," I said. "But tomorrow. Because tonight, you're going to tell us a bedtime story about dad. And I'm not going to miss it for the world."

THANK you so much for reading, Coffee & Corpses. If you enjoyed the small town of Coffee Creek, then you'll want to check out the next books in the series! Check them out HERE!

AND IF YOU want to read the story that Roberta tells Connie and Reba at the end of Coffee & Corpses, CLICK HERE to sign up for my newsletter and I'll send you that story for free!

READ THE FIRST TWO CHAPTERS
OF BOOK 2!

Thank you so much for reading Coffee & Corpses!

To read the first two chapters of the next book in the series, Ligature & Latte, just keep going!

Thanks and God Bless,
Maisy

MAISY MARPLE

LIGATURE
& LATTE

Book Two in the Connie Cafe Mystery Series

LIGATURE & LATTE CHAPTER ONE

This was the day my dreams came true!

I, Connie Cafe, was going to meet with James Popper, the best realtor in Coffee Creek.

The journey that started when I was a child, dreaming of imaginary dragons in my backyard while my father drank piping hot cups of black coffee, was about to become my reality. I was going to open my very own coffee shop in Coffee Creek.

Everything got sidetracked for me after my father died. I'd moved home to live with my mother and started working for some big chain coffee shop and getting the scoop on local stories for the *Coffee Creek Gazette*.

Long story short, a few months back, I was reporting on the Coffee Creek Golf Tournament and found David Gardner, the best golfer in Coffee Creek, dead in a water hazard. Well, timing is everything, apparently, because I was the main suspect in the case — that was until I proved my innocence.

Thankfully, that mess went away, and my mother, Roberta Cafe, encouraged me to open up my dream coffee shop in Coffee Creek. And my best friend, Reba, said she was going to come work for me.

The time was here for me to open up *Connie's Cafe* on Main Street, right in the heart of Coffee Creek!

But before I got ahead of myself, I had to find a building. That was where James came in.

"It's good to see you looking excited about something," my mother said, handing me a big mug of java as I walked into the kitchen of our old farmhouse. "It's been a while."

I nodded, accepting the dark roast with open arms. "I agree. I feel like I've been in a ten-year funk."

"Twelve," my mother winked. "But who's counting?"

"Apparently, not me."

"So, how many places are you looking at today?"

"I think James said he had three. Two of them are on Main Street, and the other one's a little off the beaten path." I rolled my eyes. "I told him that I didn't want to be anywhere other than Main Street, but he insisted. I guess you can get away with being pushy when you've got the reputation he has."

"I guess," my mother shrugged. "Just promise me one thing, honey?"

"What's that?"

"Promise me that you will make the choice that's best for you. This is your dream. Don't let someone else try to tell you how to live your life."

"As she tries to tell me how to live my life," I snorted. Coffee went flying onto the counter and farmhouse floor. I was so excited I couldn't even get the joke out without just about choking on my coffee.

"Serves you right." My mother handed me a paper towel to clean up the mess I'd made. "I'm not trying to run your life, ya know. I just want you to go out and get what you've worked so hard for, that's all."

"I know, mom." I threw the coffee-speckled paper towel away and walked over to give my mother a kiss on the top of her fiery red-haired head. "I knew what you were saying."

My phone buzzed, and the sound of computerized ducks emerged from the back pocket of my jeans.

"What in the world is that?" My mother's face was contorted into the cutest little ball of confusion I'd ever seen.

"It's my alarm," I laughed, hoping I could stifle it just a little. I'd already sprayed coffee all over the kitchen because I was making fun of the woman who gave me life. At this point, I needed to be careful, or I was going to find myself on the wrong side of cold coffee for breakfast and peanut butter and jelly sandwiches for dinner.

"Interesting fact about coffee," I said, holding a finger in the air. "If you drink it piping hot, it's delicious. If you drink it over ice and freezing cold, it's delicious. If it's anywhere in the middle of that temperature spectrum, it is completely undrinkable."

"I don't know where that's coming from," my mother smiled. "But I'm going to go ahead and disagree with you. For my money, it doesn't get any better than a cup of coffee that was poured hot but left on the counter for a few hours. That's when things really get exciting. Just my opin-ion," she said, raising her eyebrows innocently.

"Really?!?" I furrowed my brow. "How can you drink that stuff?"

"I can't!" She laughed so hard at her own joke coffee almost went flying out of *her* nose. She doubled over and began slapping her thighs. "You should have seen your face!"

"Ha, ha, very funny," I said, grabbing my keys and heading for the door. "I have to get going now, or I'm going to be late."

"Okay, honey. Good luck today."

"Thanks. I'll tell you all about it over dinner."

"Sounds good. Love you."

"Love you, too."

I parked my car about halfway down Main Street, next to the *Coffee Creek Flour & Love Bakery*.

James was across the street and about a forty-foot walk

to the northern section of the street, right next to the *Coffee Creek Post Office.*

James Popper did not disappoint, and he hadn't even shown me any properties yet.

He was dressed to the nines in a great-looking gray suit, which, given the fact that it was almost July and temps were in the mid-eighties most days, he definitely earned some extra points in my book. His shirt was a navy blue, and he had the most enticing shade of green silk tied in a double Windsor around his neck. The whole ensemble made his thick black beard and hazel eyes really pop. He kept his head shaved really smooth on top.

He was a looker, for sure!

I wasn't sure if it was James Popper's most dapper appearance, my own excitement at finally getting my cafe started, or if the building was actually as perfect as I thought, but from the moment I saw it, I thought it was *the one.*

We hadn't even gone inside yet, and I was practically drooling over it.

The building was close to the Post Office but not connected. There was a narrow alleyway between the two buildings. The shop was narrow, with a nice little patio out front.

I was already envisioning wrought-iron tables with umbrellas and cute little chairs. This area would be able to accommodate seating for four or five people, and it would give them a wonderful view of Main Street and all of the things that were going on. It was the perfect spot for sipping coffee and people-watching while enjoying great conversation and a perfectly baked pastry.

As I brought my eyes to the building itself, the first thing that caught my attention were the two massive windows that flanked each side of the door. What a great place to have local artwork or advertise menu items that would draw people in. Plus, they were big enough that people walking by could see how inviting things were inside.

"It's perfect!" I announced to James. It was hard for me to keep from jumping up and down right there on the sidewalk.

"Well, don't you want to see it first?" He asked. "That's generally how we do things in the Real Estate business."

He held out a coffee with my name on it. I recognized Reba's handwriting and thought *girl, you're not going to be working there much longer, I promise.*

"Of course," I nodded. "I'm just a tad more than a little excited about getting started."

"I understand," he said, taking a hit off his steaming cup. "Please don't think I'm overstepping here, but it'll be to your benefit to take a deep breath and try to take the emotion out of it while you're looking. It would be a shame for you to buy a building that you were really excited about, only to find out later that it doesn't suit your needs the way you thought it would."

"That's a good point," I said, holding my cup up. "Thanks for the coffee, by the way."

"You're welcome. I didn't know what kind you liked, but the girl at the counter said you like dark roast, black as black can be. Honestly, I don't even know how she knew who I was getting coffee for."

"That's Reba," I smiled. "I told her I was meeting with you today, and she absolutely steered you in the right direction."

We stood in front of the building, drinking coffee for a moment. James was clearly in no hurry to move. It was starting to feel a bit awkward when I asked, "Are you going to show me the inside?"

"Oh, sure," he said. "I was just trying to give you the feel of what your future customers might be experiencing in this location. As you sip your coffee, look around at what's going on. Is this what you'd want for them? If it is, then maybe this is the place for you. If it's not, is there something you could do to fix it? Or would you be stuck with it as it is?"

This guy was good. I'd never thought about asking myself all of these questions. Certainly, I'd imagined my own dream scenario, but now as I looked around, I noticed a large tree that overhung the patio. I'd have to sweep leaves and acorns out of the way every day. The patio was only about ten feet from the street, and anyone sitting out there would have their view entirely blocked if a car were to park directly in front of the shop, which would inevitably happen as Main Street was crowded in the summer.

"Thank you," I said, turning to him and noticing what a punch his hazel eyes packed. "I wasn't thinking like that at all. I can definitely see some issues with this place."

"Very good. Now, we're going to go inside. I want you to think about all of the things you're going to need to set up your front of house the way you want it. Is there going to be enough counter space? Will you have enough room for patrons to be comfortable and enjoy their stay, or would you need more space? Is the kitchen area going to give you enough space for the equipment you're going to need?"

He opened the door, and I stepped into the space. At that moment, I was so thankful that God had sent James Popper to Coffee Creek. His reputation was well-earned. He didn't just want to sell me a building, make his money, and get out. It was clear that he wanted me to have the best building for me. He wanted *Connie's Cafe* to be the best it could be.

As I stepped over the threshold, I could feel a darkness about this place that I wasn't sure any amount of paint or fancy lighting would be able to fix.

"I can't thank you enough," I said. "I was ready to plunk down my money and settle into this place today. But your encouragement to look for flaws has been a real eye-opener."

"Well, we have two other places to look at today. All of

these places are going to have things you won't like. But as you look at them, start to think about which flaws you can live with and which ones are going to be too problematic to overcome."

"I will," I said, moving through the main area and into the kitchen. It was tiny and cramped, and there was no way I was going to be able to do what I wanted to do back here.

The clincher came when I looked out the back door. There was another building, big and brick, within ten feet. This meant that the only place for people to have their coffee was the patio out front or the dimly lit area inside.

This place was not the one. It's funny how slowing down for just a few minutes was enough to completely open my eyes enough to prevent me from making a major mistake.

I wrinkled my nose and looked at James. "This is not the place for me."

He nodded and gave me a wink. "Very good, grasshopper. You have mastered lesson one. Let's go see what lesson two has in store for us."

LIGATURE & LATTE CHAPTER TWO

James and I crossed the street and started walking toward the south side of Main Street. The second property of the day was on the creek side of the street, which made me quite happy.

"I don't want to steer you or get your expectations too high, but I really think you're going to enjoy this next place a lot more than you did the first."

"We'll see," I said playfully.

"Yes," He nodded. "We will."

We were about halfway there when we passed *Coffee Creek Antiques & Valuables.* Mable Wilson, the owner, came out of the front door in a flurry.

"You've got some nerve!" She cried out. She was waving a rolled-up newspaper.

We both turned to see the seventy-five-year-old, whose wrinkles and white hair made her look much older. She was wearing a pair of loose brown pants and a knitted blue sweater, which hung on her.

"James Popper, you're going to have to answer to someone for this!"

"I'm sorry, Mable." His voice was calm, but I noticed that a few beads of sweat were forming on his forehead. "I have no idea what you're talking about?"

"I'm talking about bringing that murderer around here," she said, not mincing any words.

"Murderer?" James asked. "Mable, Connie's not a murderer. She's been proven innocent of all that stuff. She simply wants to move on with her life and start a new business in Coffee Creek. That's all."

Mable shot me a glance. "You stay right there," she said to me. "I'm warning you, don't come to a step closer." If we hadn't been in the middle of Main Street, with other people starting to get out and about for the day, I probably would have laughed a little bit at the absurdity of this whole situation. As it was, there were people starting to poke their heads out of the various shops, and this situation was not really very funny anymore … if it had ever been.

Then she opened up a newspaper from the previous month. There I was, on the front page, a horrible photo of me and a headline and article that were full of lies.

It caught me by surprise. I, honestly, thought those papers had all been thrown away.

"Mable," I said, finding my voice. "I've already been proven innocent of David Gardner's murder. It wasn't me at all."

"I don't believe that for a second." She spat on the sidewalk next to her foot. "Once a killer, always a killer." She turned her attention back to James. "And if you help her get a place down here with us honest, do-gooders, then heaven help you for what your fate may be."

James shook his head and blinked his eyes a few times, not really sure what to say to Mable.

"Mable," he finally replied. "You have a good day. I'm going to take Connie, who didn't kill anyone, by the way, to go look at another place."

He touched my arm and guided me gently. It was reassuring to have him there. I didn't know how I would have handled the exchange if it had just been me.

This is what I had been afraid of once those articles started coming out. I knew that most people would be able to understand that I hadn't done anything wrong. But I also knew that there would be others.

Unfortunately, Mable was one of those others. She had a reputation for being a rather loud gossip. Her circle was small, but they were vicious. She'd made more than a few stinks in her years, and there was one thing that I'd grown to know about Mable.

If she wanted her way, she was going to get it.

TRYING to forget the public derision at the tongue of Mable Wilson, James and I continued on to the next place on the list.

It was a tall brick building with a nice wide storefront and those big showy windows on both sides of the door.

I noticed right away that if I were to buy this building, then *Connie's Cafe* would be feet away from *Coffee Creek Reads & Teas*. I thought that this might be a very good thing. For one, tea wouldn't be on my menu. And for another, what goes better with a great book than coffee?

Nothing.

Taking a deep breath, I started to calm myself down and look around the area, taking in all of the possibilities and potential roadblocks.

The first real drawback was that I was only two doors down from that awful Mable Wilson and her antique shop. I wasn't sure that there was a place I could find that would be far enough away from her.

The second drawback I noticed was that with this building, there was no place for outside seating. The building went right up to the edge of the sidewalk, which left no room for tables and chairs as it would be in the way of people passing by, making an unpleasant experience for everyone.

"I see you looking around for outside seating capabilities," James interrupted my thoughts.

I smiled.

"That's okay," he said. "There's a surprise on the back of this building that will take care of all of your outdoor seating needs." He flashed me a grin that just about melted me.

"Ooooh", I squealed, rubbing the palms of my hands together.

Before we went in to inspect further, Rebecca Fairmack, the owner of *Coffee Creek Teas & Reads,* came out to join us.

She was a spunky little pocket of energy. She had bright blond hair, bright pink glasses, and a very chic little pastel blue dress. She was wearing orange and yellow flip-flops and drinking tea out of a mug that read: *I am a Reading & Tea Kinda Girl.* The mug had a picture of an open book and a cup of tea on the front of it.

"Hey there, Connie!" She said. Her voice was as sunny and bright as her outfit and hair. "Hi, James!"

"Hey there, Rebecca," James said. "How are things in the book and tea business going?"

She nodded, "Can't complain. People love to read and drink tea."

"That they do," James agreed. "So Connie here is going to be looking at this building here next to yours."

"Welcome to the neighborhood," Rebecca giggled.

"Thank you," I said.

Having a neighbor like Rebecca was a major positive to this second building. She was kind and upbeat, and I was already starting to think about ways that we could work together to make a really great experience for the readers and coffee drinkers of Coffee Creek.

A young couple turned into *Reads & Teas*.

"I've got to go, but we'll catch up later." She went back inside her shop. I was glad she'd come out to greet us. Her visit gave me a completely rejuvenated feeling of the Main Street vibe. I could work with her, no problem.

"Shall we," James said, bringing my focus back to the place in front of us.

"Yes," I grinned. "We shall."

THE PLACE WAS ABSOLUTELY PERFECT. The inside seating area was spacious and open, with bright hardwood floors and a nice shade of orange on the walls. This side of the street got the morning sun which made this space bright and vibrant.

The existing counters were exactly what I'd dreamt about for years. They were long and extensive, allowing for ample room for a register area, serving area, and coffee preparation area. The back counter had a great deal of space for all of the equipment, plus there was a built-in sink for quick and easy cleaning of blenders and coffee pots.

There was already a glass display case for pastries and other baked goods.

"The seller said all of the equipment in here is included in the asking price," James informed me.

"Very nice," I nodded. "I like all of this so far. I know this place is the most expensive of the three, but if I don't have to spend a ton of money on extra equipment, it might be worth shelling out a little more."

"That's what I was thinking," James flashed me that smile again, and I felt goosebumps starting on my arms. "Let's go see the kitchen."

It was a much larger kitchen than the previous place. It had full working ovens and a nice prep table in the middle, with plenty of room to move around, even if several people were back there working.

"I love this place!" I was like a child on Christmas morning, rushing downstairs and finding that Santa had brought exactly what I'd asked for. "James, I'm going to be honest with you. I don't even want to look at the third place."

He grinned. "I haven't even shown you the best part of this one yet."

I followed him out of the kitchen and back into the main area. Along the back wall there was a door that led up three steps and out onto a massive deck. There had to have been room for at least twenty tables out here. It had the most beautiful view of Coffee Creek.

The sun was glistening off the water as the birds were

flying high in the sky and the fish were jumping. I felt the warmth of the sun on my back, filling me with the happy feelings I knew my customers would someday feel when they sat out here.

"I'll take it!"

Tap Here To Continue Reading

ALSO BY MAISY MARPLE

Visit Maisy Marple's Author Page on Amazon to read any of the titles below!

Connie Cafe Series

Coffee & Corpses

Ligature & Latte

Autumn & Autopsies

Pumpkins & Poison

Death & Decaf

Turkey & Treachery

Mistletoe & Memories

Snow & Sneakery

Repairs & Renovations

Bagels & Bible Study

S'more Jesus

Proverbs & Preparations

Sharpe & Steele Series

Beachside Murder

Sand Dune Slaying

Boardwalk Body Parts

RV Resort Mystery Series

Campground Catastrophe

Bad News Barbecues

Sunsets and Bad Bets

Short Stories

Forty Years Together

Long Story Short

The Best Gift of All

Miracle at the Mall

The Ornament

The Christmas Cabin

Cold Milk at Midnight

Short Story Collections

Hot Cocoa Christmas

Unapologetically Christian Essays

Reason for the Season

God is Not Santa Claus

Free Will is Messy

Fear Not

Not About this World

We Are All Broken

Veritas

God Ain't Your Butler

An Argument for Hate

Agape Love (With Pastor Michael Golden)

<u>Addiction Help</u>

Hard Truths: Overcoming Alcoholism One Second At A Time

ABOUT THE AUTHOR

Maisy Marple is a lover of small town cozy mysteries, plus she has a wicked coffee habit to boot. She loves nothing more than diving into a clean mystery with a cup of the darkest, blackest coffee around.

She grew up in a small town and now lives in the country, giving her more than enough inspiration for creating the cozy locales and memorable characters that are on display in her Connie Cafe Mystery Series!

To connect with Maisy, sign up for her VIP reader list and get a free mystery story. Check out the offer on the previous page.

Made in United States
Troutdale, OR
12/11/2024

26306765R00119